# ONCE UPON A CAMEL

## ALSO BY KATHI APPELT

*Angel Thieves*

*Counting Crows*

*Keeper*

*Max Attacks*

*Maybe a Fox* (with Alison McGhee)

*Mogie*

*The True Blue Scouts of Sugar Man Swamp*

*The Underneath*

# Once Upon a
# CAMEL

**KATHI APPELT**

Pictures by **ERIC ROHMANN**

*A Caitlyn Dlouhy Book*

Atheneum Atheneum Books for Young Readers

New York  London  Toronto  Sydney  New Delhi

ATHENEUM BOOKS FOR YOUNG READERS • An imprint of Simon & Schuster Children's Publishing Division • 1230 Avenue of the Americas, New York, New York 10020 • This book is a work of fiction. Any references to historical events, real people, or real places are used fictitiously. Other names, characters, places, and events are products of the author's imagination, and any resemblance to actual events or places or persons, living or dead, is entirely coincidental. • Text © 2021 by Kathi Appelt • Cover illustration © 2021 by Eric Rohmann • Cover design by Greg Stadnyk © 2021 by Simon & Schuster, Inc. • Interior illustrations © 2021 by Eric Rohmann • All rights reserved, including the right of reproduction in whole or in part in any form. • ATHENEUM BOOKS FOR YOUNG READERS is a registered trademark of Simon & Schuster, Inc. Atheneum logo is a trademark of Simon & Schuster, Inc. • For information about special discounts for bulk purchases, please contact Simon & Schuster Special Sales at 1-866-506-1949 or business@simonandschuster.com. • The Simon & Schuster Speakers Bureau can bring authors to your live event. For more information or to book an event, contact the Simon & Schuster Speakers Bureau at 1-866-248-3049 or visit our website at www.simonspeakers.com. • Also available in an Atheneum Books for Young Readers hardcover edition • Interior design by Irene Metaxatos • The text for this book was set in Excelsior LT Std • The illustrations for this book were rendered in oil paint. • Manufactured in the United States of America • 0323 MTN • First Atheneum Books for Young Readers paperback edition September 2022 • 10  9  8  7  6  5  4  3 • The Library of Congress has cataloged the hardcover edition as follows: • Names: Appelt, Kathi, 1954– author. | Rohmann, Eric, illustrator. • Title: Once upon a camel / Kathi Appelt ; illustrated by Eric Rohmann. • Description: First edition. | New York : Atheneum Books for Young Readers, [2021] | Audience: Ages 8–12. | Audience: Grades 4–6. | Summary: In 1910, Zada the camel treks across the West Texas desert to save two baby kestrels from an approaching haboob, a mountain-sized storm, sharing adventures from her youth in Turkey to keep them calm. • Identifiers: LCCN 2020056516 | ISBN 9781534406438 (hardcover) | ISBN 9781534406445 (pbk) | ISBN 9781534406452 (ebook) • Subjects: CYAC: Camels—Fiction. | Kestrels—Fiction. | Animals—Infancy—Fiction. | Dust storms—Fiction. | Storytelling—Fiction. | Texas—History—1865–1950—Fiction. | Turkey—History—Abdul Mejid, 1839–1861—Fiction. • Classification: LCC PZ7.A6455 Onc 2021 | DDC [Fic]—dc23 • LC record available at https://lccn.loc.gov/2020056516

*For my darling Emma—*
*With love,*
*—K. A.*

*For Kathi,*
*thanks for reminding me look up*
*at the night sky*
*—E. R.*

# ONCE UPON A CAMEL

# 1

## Foothills, Chisos Mountains West Texas

### 1910

"Incoming!"

Even in her sleep, Zada recognized that voice.

The old camel raised one eyelid. It was still dark. There was at least an hour left before dawn. She did not recall setting an early alarm bird.

Zada settled deeper into her sandy furrow, yawned. But before she could drift back off, here it came, a high-speed bundle of flapping kestrel feathers. American kestrel to be specific, smallest of the falcon family; and it barreled directly

toward Zada's face. Peck-peck-peck. Ouch ouch OUCH!

"Zada! Wake up!"

Perlita!

In a pecking frenzy! Ouch, ouch, ouch and more ouch! Any chance for more sleep was now fully dashed.

"Zada!" Perlita said. "It's the *worst* news."

Perlita did a hoppity-hoppity dance on Zada's nose. Then she puffed herself up, so anxious she could hardly contain herself.

Zada waited.

Perlita puffed.

Long pause.

More puffing.

Long pause number two.

Puff-puff-puff.

Long pause number 5,863.

Extreme puffing.

Finally Zada couldn't stand it. "Chirp it out!" she said.

At last Perlita, still maximally puffed, cut loose with a dizzying trail of words that quickly turned into a torrent, which she strung together into an array of *klee*s and *killy*s. As best Zada could make out, Perlita's monologue went something like . . .

"There's a mountain . . .

". . . coming toward us . . .

". . . a huge, HUGE, mountain . . .

". . . the TALLEST in history . . .

". . . and it's so big . . . and so tall . . .

". . . it's taking up the entire world . . .

". . . the entire universe.

"And it's moving our way."

Perlita's voice had gone so fevered that it made Zada wince, even without the message that was attached to it. And the message was *It's going to eat us, Zada. I'm telling you. There's a mountain coming our way. It's sucking everything into its bigbigbig behemoth belly.*

Zada looked around. It was still dark, but she

could tell by the thin rays of the dawn's early light that the Chisos sat squarely in the same places they'd always sat. She could see their peaks, right where they should be, just below the stars.

"I don't see anything," said Zada, trying to fathom what on earth had ruffled Perlita's feathers.

"You can't see it from here," said Perlita, her distress growing by the second. "It's coming across the canyon."

"The canyon?" asked Zada. From their vantage point near the creek, the canyon was hidden behind a set of ridges and a wide plateau. Ordinarily, Zada avoided the canyon. When she stood at the top of it and stared down at its steep, jagged walls, it made her dizzy; standing at the bottom of it and looking up at its steep, jagged walls, she got woozy.

Of course, a canyon is not a problem for a kestrel. Perlita flew over it all the time, which was how she had spotted the moving mountain, which she was sure was going to eat them, which made her . . . Peck-peck-peck.

"Ouch." Zada wrinkled her nose.

"Oh, sorry," said Perlita, catching herself mid-frenzy. A tuft of camel fur was caught on the side of her beak. She flapped into the air and *zzzzzziiiippppp* . . . she buzzed again, first one way, then the other, then she shot straight up, banked, and made a death-defying midair U-turn . . . *zzzziiiippppp* . . . she buzzed back the other way and paused in front of Zada's face only long enough to say, "The mountain! It's eating everything, even the stars!"

"But Perlita . . ." Zada tried to follow her flight, when *zing!*, a second blurry object blew by her face.

Pard! Perlita's one and only. He zoomed by so fast he made the stars blink.

Then he circled back and landed right between the camel's eyes. "Zada!" he exclaimed. "There's a mountain! It's going to eat us!"

6

# Foothills, Chisos Mountains
# West Texas
**1910**

Zada knew that there were any number of things that ate tiny kestrels, as well as a few that ate large camels.

Mountain *lions*? Maybe. Bears? Possible. Wolves? It could happen.

Mountains? No.

From her customary spot next to the cotton-wood tree, she checked out the kestrels' nest, a cavity chiseled there by a ladder-back woodpecker who had abandoned it years ago. Even in the dimness, she could not see anything amiss. Nary a nest robber in sight. Not a kit fox. Not a coach-whip. Nada. *In fact*, nothing was moving.

This was usually the time of dawn when the black-tailed jackrabbits emerged from their dens to graze on the surrounding vervain and persimmon plants. Normally, Zada could see the shadows of their giant ears, bopping from one stand of sage to another. But just then? Nope.

Ordinarily, she could hear the snuffle of the javelinas, rummaging for an early breakfast through the shrubby patches to the west. Again, nothing.

Zada cocked her ears. There was no melancholy howling of the local song dogs, not a single, solitary note afloat, much less the usual dawn chorus.

Where was everybody?

Just then, the wind did an unexpected dance. From near stillness, it picked itself up. *Nip! Nip! Nip!* Tiny pricks of sand blew under Zada's coat.

A willy-willy tugged at her chin, followed by another that bumped against her side. The willy-willies were mostly invisible. *Mostly harmless,* thought Zada.

But then she felt another . . . and another . . . and one more . . .

Zada knew: don't underestimate a willy-willy. They stay low, then *whoosh!* they grow and grow and grow until they become:

> dust devils,
>
> simoons,
>
> samiels.

And they, in turn, become something larger still.

# Foothills, Chisos Mountains
# West Texas
## 1910

Zada looked back in the direction of the canyon. Where there should have been a whole blanket of fading stars, there was—oh no!—only a curtain of dark, dark brown!

In that horrible moment Zada realized: coming toward them wasn't a moving mountain, even though it looked like one. She knew exactly what this was: a haboob, a wall of dust and sand. She also knew it could doze down the shrubs and cholla and mesquites and even the mighty Spanish daggers that ruled over all the other desert shrubs.

Like a tsunami. But instead of an enormous wave of water, she saw a gigantic wave of dust. Higher than any of the surrounding peaks, including Casa Grande. And it was gaining speed; it wouldn't take long for it to reach Zada and her kestrel companions.

She looked to the cottonwood nest, where Pard and Perlita now sat shivering. The old tree would normally be a perfectly fine place to ride out a storm. After all, it had survived a century or more of growing there. But a haboob was different. The roiling dust could suffocate most everything, including the nest's feathered inhabitants.

Now, a camel is designed for the desert. She has an inner eyelid and extra-long eyelashes for keeping the sand out of her eyes. She can close her nostrils in order to filter out the dust when she breathes. Even her rounded ears can divert the blowing sand. Made to withstand dust storms, that's Zada. Not so much with kestrels. But at least they could fly up and over it. Couldn't they?

Then two of them—Perlita and Pard, to be exact—in a single voice, shouted, "We have to evacuate the babies!"

The babies! Zada's heart gave a bang. How could she have forgotten?

Wims and Beulah, small round fluff balls, hardly bigger than purple thistle blossoms. They were barely two weeks old. Aside from a few sprouting feathers, they still had their baby down. They certainly hadn't fledged yet.

Zada's heart banged harder: How were the chicks supposed to evacuate if they couldn't fly?

As if Perlita could read her mind, she said, "You'll have to give them a ride."

Of course! After all, no small number of birds had hitchhiked on her back through the years. They usually landed right on her hump. Once perched, they helped themselves to the sand fleas that were lodged beneath her camel coat. The bird got a ride and a snack and Zada got some relief from the fleas. It was a win-win. Perlita herself had taken many such rides.

Zada was about to give the O.O.D. (Official Okie Dokie), but then a bead of worry scurried down her neck. Whenever the ride got too bumpy, Perlita could just hop up and fly away. But Wims and Beulah? Without sufficient wing power yet? All at once Zada realized: Everything would depend upon their baby toes, and their gripping abilities. But how strong were baby bird toes anyways?

"We have to get to the Mission," said Perlita, interrupting Zada's thoughts.

The Mission? The Mission was a good refuge, but it had been years since Zada had last been there. It would mean trekking across rough terrain. And though Zada had walked many . . . no . . . thousands of miles across the hot, burning sand, she was not the nimble young *Camelus dromedarius* she had once been. Her knees were creakier than ever. Her stamina was not at all staminus.

Could she even make it?

Before she could answer that question . . . from the depths of the nest, she heard *peep peep peep*. It was the universal language of all baby birds.

"Klee, klee," whistled Perlita. One worried mama.

"Killy, killy," chirped Pard. One desperate dad.

"Peeppeeppeeppeeppeeppeep!" cried Beulah and Wims. Two adorable bambinos.

In the midst of all this, she heard, "Zada-ZadaZadaZada!" Riding on the currents above her head was a cloud of panicked black-chinned hummingbirds, their invisible wings whirring through the air.

"ZadaZadaZada," they chirred. "Ruuuunnnn! The mountain is moving."

Again, the question *Could she make it?* buzzed through her head and formed a cloud around her brain. She blinked her eyes, tried to clear it. *Well,* she thought, *we are about to find out.* "Binicileri getirin!" she said, and slowly . . . slowly . . . oh, so slowly . . . she raised her back end, followed by her front. The morning air always made her joints a little sticky. Lately, getting up and down took a major effort. Finally, all seven feet of her, from the bottom of her toes to the top of her hump, stood atop the desert floor.

She gave her coat a great shake, sending sand flying in every direction. Then, with three long strides, she was at the cottonwood. Now she had to convince Beulah and Wims to hop onto her head. She leaned against the tree's rough bark, raised her head until it was just underneath the opening of the nest, and with as much good cheer as she could muster, she urged, "All aboard, young kestrels." Inside, Perlita and Pard worked to coax the babies toward the opening and onto the camel's noggin.

"I'm scared," said Wims.

"Me too," said Beulah.

And that was followed by . . . *peeppeep-peeppeeppeeppeeppeeppeeppeeppeeppeeppeep-peep . . . !!!!*

"Hey now, hey now," said Zada, in her most reassuring voice, which wasn't all that reassuring because . . . *haboob*!

"Hop on," she said. The wind nudged up against her.

A squadron of willy-willies swirled by.

"Time is wasting . . ."

*Peeppeeppeepeeppeeppeeppeeppeeppeep-peeppeeppeeppeeppeeppeep . . . !!!!!*

But the chicks wouldn't budge.

Not. One. Inch. Meter. Foot. Mile. Nary a budge was in the offing.

What was in the offing was a growing panic. Zada knew a thing or two about that. She searched her memory. . . . There was a word she needed. . . . It was right on the tip of her tongue. . . . No, it was a phrase. . . .

"Hurry," said Perlita.

"We've got to go!" shouted Pard.

Zada closed her eyes. What could she say to convince the chicks to move?

*Pip-pip?* No, not important enough.

*Step on it?* Not right either.

*Get on, or else?* Absolutely not.

"Ah!" she exclaimed. "I remember!"

Quickly, she whispered to the chicks, "En parlak yildiz ol." It was an old saying, one from her earliest memories, one that she would explain later.

Fortunately, for just that second, thanks to all that is good and right, the chicks seemed to understand, if not the meaning, at least the promise of the words.

They tucked their not-ready-for-flight wings against their pudgy bodies, checked their peeps, and with a single hop, did a perfect two-chick landing, right into the thick tuft on top of Zada's head, wrapped their toes around her fur, and clung with all their mini-avian might.

## Foothills, Chisos Mountains West Texas

**1910**

If only Perlita and Pard had kept their wings tucked too, all *would* have been hunky-dory. But even smart birds will instinctively stretch out their wings when they jump. And that was a major mistake. Instead of the kestrels landing next to their chicks atop Zada's head, where there was just enough room to make a temporary nest for the whole crew, a stray dust devil blew up from beneath, grabbed the pair in its blustery fist, and rocketed them into the sky.

"Noooo!!!" shouted Zada.

"Mommy!" cried the chicks, gripping the fur between Zada's ears. "Daddy!" But their urgent voices were no match for the dust devil.

As Zada and the babies watched, the wind whirled Perlita and Pard into feathery specks, no bigger than motes.

Then *poof!* just like that, it carried them high, high into the sky and erased them altogether.

"Come back, come back, come back," cried Beulah and Wims.

Zada gasped. Perlita and Pard had been right in front of her, right in front of the chicks, and then they weren't.

"Klee, klee, klee," called Wims.

"Killy, killy," Beulah cried.

Zada lifted her head away from the tree, careful not to tip it too far back. Maybe, she thought, if they stood there, Perlita and Pard would magically drop out of the sky. But there was no sign of them. Just the darkening clouds of dust, circling, swirling, blocking the rising sun.

# Foothills, Chisos Mountains
# West Texas
**1910**

*Killy, killy. Klee, klee.* The more the babies called, the more the wind blew. Faster and faster it whirled. The twins would never be able to withstand the power of a haboob, Zada knew, no matter how hard they held on. Sharp pricks of sand began to pummel at them as the twosome burrowed deeper into her thick fur.

Zada had to get ahead of this wind, find some shelter. Perlita had said to head to the Mission, but at the rate the dust cloud was moving toward them, there was no way they could make it there before the storm caught them. Not for the first time in her long life, Zada wished she could fly.

Other animals raced past. Jackrabbits. Quail. A pair of bears. There was even a swarm of grasshoppers flittering by. They all had one thing on their minds: shelter.

But where? *Think, Zada. Think, think, think.* They had to find a way station.

"Auntie Zada," cried Wims.

"Where are we going?" asked Beulah.

"Well," she said, wishing she knew. "If we were badgers, we'd burrow into a deep hole underneath the ground."

"But we're not badgers!" Beulah said crossly.

"If we were fish," Zada said next, "we'd swim down the river, where no dust could get us." Of course, none of them were fish, so that was a nonstarter too. But where, Zada, where could an old

21

camel with two fluffy kestral passengers go to get out of the way of a moving mountain?

As Beulah informed her that they most certainly were not fish, somehow, amid all the clamor, *kllloookkll, kllloookkll*. Sweet, but barely there; a sound she hadn't heard in years.

She stopped, flicked her ear.

*Kllloookkll*. There it was again. The faint ringing of a bell. Like the coo of a pigeon. She leaned toward it, listened. But as quickly as it came, it disappeared, leaving only the thrum of the increasing rush of the haboob, coming on fast. *A trick of the wind,* Zada thought. But a trick was not what she needed. Shelter—that was the goal. *Concentrate, Zada.* All at once, she remembered: a shallow cave.

The escarpment. Yes!

She knew how to get there. It wasn't that far! No more than a mile; two at most. It would do until the storm passed and they could continue to the Mission, where, once Perlita and Pard blew down from wherever they'd blown up to, the two parent birds would think to meet them.

Zada and the chicks would be their own caravan. *A caravan of three,* she thought.

How long had it been, Zada couldn't help but wonder, since she'd last traveled in a caravan? She thought about her old camel compadres. *Asiye. Halime. Naime. Rezan. Tarkan. Kahraman. Elif. Melek.* Ending with her own name, *Zada.* Always with their cameleer, Teodor. No matter how hard the path, or how long the trail, Teodor would sing their names out loud. Over and over, in a chant, nine altogether.

Which was what Zada did now. She sang out the old names, old friends, as loud as she could in the roaring wind, sang them in time to her careful steps.

And it was almost as if they were all right there beside her, urging her on, when *whoosh*, a stray downdraft shoved against her. She swaaaaaayyyed to the left, then swaaaaaayyyed

23

to the right, from one side to another and back. She took in a deep breath and waited for the wind to pass by.

"Auntie!" cried the chicks, alarmed. Then: "Where's Mommy? I want Daddy. I'm scared. Me too." And of course, *pppeeeepppeeeepppeeeeepppeeeeep!*

Zada dug her feet into the sand to brace herself. "Hey now, hey now," she said, trying to keep her voice steady, even though nothing about her felt steady at all. "We are not badgers or fish. We are caravanners!"

And Beulah, bless her, said in her bravest voice, "I think I always wanted to be a caravanner."

"Me too," said Wims. "I want to be a caravanner too."

And with that, the threesome leaned into the wind. "To the escarpment," said Zada. Tallyho!

# 6

## Mountain Lion Territory

**1910**

The escarpment would give them a respite on their journey, for sure. But what Zada did not tell the babies was that there might be one slightly huge problem: Pecos de Leon, the resident mountain lion.

Zada had first met Pecos de Leon when he was just a cub. He had been adorable then, but that was years ago, and now, Zada thought, adorable would not accurately capture his personality.

Like the wind, he was elusive, slinking between the arches and arroyos, his tawny coat a perfect disguise against the sandstone walls. Unless you knew that you were looking at a mountain lion, you could mistake him for one of the many rocks or boulders that littered the landscape.

Nevertheless, in their few encounters, Zada and Pecos had maintained a certain amount of respect for each other, thanks to their shared history. They had both traveled a lot of miles and traversed a lot of country. That was worth something.

More than once, Zada had spotted Pecos lounging in front of the escarpment. But a mountain lion's territory is wide. Today, if she was lucky, he'd be on the far side of his range. If she wasn't lucky, maybe, hopefully, he wouldn't be hungry. Mountain lion or not, the escarpment was their best chance, at least as a temporary measure.

"Hang on, bird scouts," she told the babies.

Stretching her long neck—her racing stance— she set out, taking each step with caution, care-

26

ful not to stumble. She couldn't risk Wims and Beulah tumbling out.

As if they were waiting to grab one of the chicks, the willy-willies and the dust devils, the samiels and simoons, danced all around Zada. They swiped at her ankles, raced ahead of her, rose and fell, then rose and fell again, reminding her of the ocean's waves.

Zada. Ship of the desert, as a camel is known, picked her way past them, while the sun and the very last of the morning stars blinked out one at a time in the disappearing sky.

# Mountain Lion Territory
## 1910

American kestrels are custom-built for aerodynamics. They're among the bird kingdom's most agile raptors. They can ride comfortably on the upper wind currents for hours at a time, and upon spotting a grasshopper or a mouse from a thousand feet up, they can dive at speeds that astonish, over two hundred miles per hour.

Despite it all, Zada couldn't help but worry about Perlita and Pard. No matter their agility, they would be no match for the haboob. Blasting sand can strip paint from buildings. It can scrape the rust off metal. What could it do to a pair of birds?

As if to make the point, from behind her came a horrifying *CRRRRAAAAAACCCKKKK!* The cottonwood tree! Quickly, she glanced over her shoulder. The wind had yanked it up by its roots. A hundred years, that old tree had stood there, watching over the creek, keeping generations of bird families safe. Now it lay in a heap on its side.

*Hurry, Zada, hurry!* She picked up her pace, all the while keeping her ears tuned for the sounds of Perlita's voice. But no matter how shrill the kestrels' *klees* and *killys* were, everything was drowned out in the increasing ferocity of the haboob. The wind dazzled, threw fistfuls of stinging dust at her hindquarters. She hurried.

The chicks gripped hard at her fur. Not only had they just witnessed the disappearance of their parents, but this was their very first time out of the nest.

Ever.

Zada pushed forward, the wind shoving her from behind. She held her head as steady as she could to keep the chicks from sliding.

Step, step, step, step. She didn't have time to turn around, to take stock of the haboob, no time for pausing. She didn't have to see it to know that the moving mountain was catching up to her. She could hear its roar.

Alas, Pecos de Leon had quite a roar as well. Whenever the night was quiet, Zada could hear his yowls and growls, even from miles away. Pecos was a loner. He would not appreciate her presence in his territory. He'd appreciate even less her presence in his *lair*. She sent thought beams out into the air. *Please don't be home. Please don't be home.* If he was, she'd just keep walking. There was another canyon that could provide shelter, but it was at least another mile away, over an ancient bed of lava rocks that were unnervingly wobbly, even without a pair of kestrel chicks aboard.

She thought it again: *Please don't be home.* And she hoped like crazy that somehow the big cat would get her message.

**8**

# Somewhere, Texas

## 1910

Someone else was sending a message. In fact, two someone elses were sending a message. Even as they were being tossed and spun and pummeled by the storm, Perlita and Pard called out, "Keep them safe!"

It's the universal prayer of every mother and father in every land, no matter how strong the wind, no matter how far it carried them away. No matter.

And Zada, old camel, she didn't need to hear their message to receive it.

Wasn't she the fledglings' Honorary Auntie? Had she not waited and waited and waited for them to hatch from their pebble-sized shells? And once they did, had she not watched over them every waking moment? Had she not counted each of their toes about a million times, just because it seemed like babies should have their toes counted?

Why, yes, yes, and yes to all of the above.

In fact, Zada would do anything for her bird herd. They were, after all, the only herd she now had. But knowing that didn't make the missing she felt deep inside—the missing she'd felt for at least a decade?—any less real.

And with that, the memory of her old friend Asiye flashed through her mind. Asiye. Stablemate. Fellow caravanner. Friend.

# 9

# Mountain Lion Territory

**1910**

As Zada pushed on, all around her the denizens of the desert continued to rush past. A dozen white-tailed deer. A squadron of peccaries, their squeals making Zada want to close up her ears. Others ran by in pairs: bobcats, a gray fox and her kit, armadillos. Above her head, flocks of birds—blue grosbeaks, doves, yellow-breasted chats, painted buntings—flew as fast as they could, their desperate cries punching through the roar of the wind.

Hurry, hurry, hurry.

Zada's sides heaved. Her chest burned. The sand bit into the backs of her legs, harder and harder.

Step, step, step . . . hurry, hurry, hurry. Step, step, step.

At last! Just when she thought the haboob would overtake them . . . there it was. The escarpment. The lion's lair looked to Zada like a giant mouth, carved into the rock. The scent of lion was unmistakable; every strand of fur on her large body stood up. It was such a huge risk. . . . It didn't go unnoticed to Zada that all the other animals were hurrying by, not daring to invoke the wrath—or the teeth and claws—of Pecos de Leon.

Nevertheless, it was a chance she had to take. She ducked her head to keep the chicks from being scraped by the upper edge of the rock and stepped just inside the opening. The whiskers on her lips quivered.

Another few feet, another couple of inches . . .

She waited for her eyes to adjust to the darkness, squinted. All the corners were shadow-filled. She could only barely make out the nooks and crannies that lined the inner wall.

Empty. They were all empty. No sign of Pecos. *Whew!*

Her pounding heart began to slow down. Well, as slow as it could get when the wind sounded as if a thousand longhorn cattle were stampeding all around them. Zada's ears ached with the noise of it.

But they also ached from this: *Peeppeeppeep-peeppeeppeeppeeppeeppeeppeeppeepp!*

"Caravanners," said Zada to Beulah and Wims. "We made it." She tried to sound reassuring, which was hard over the hubbub of the haboob. "We are good here," she shouted. And that was mostly true. They were out of the wind, the lion was nowhere to be seen.

Nevertheless . . . *Peeppeeppeeppeeppeeppeep-peeppeeppeep!*

"Excuse me," she said, as loudly as she could without setting off even more peep alarms. She stepped a bit farther toward the back of the cave. Ahh, thankfully, the sound of the wind was muffled there.

The chicks relaxed their grip on her tuft. Oof, that felt better. A tiny thread of peace nestled in, but not before another worry popped up. Surely the chicks must be hungry, yes? Camels can go a long time without food or water. Not so growing birdlets. From watching Perlita and Pard take turns feeding them, it seemed to Zada that baby kestrels pretty much ate all the time.

Fortunately, she had a whole cache of sand fleas in her coat, not to mention a tick or two. The supply wasn't necessarily infinite, but for now, the fleas would be enough to avert the hunger pangs. Water would be a different matter, but she couldn't worry about that until the time came. One problem at a time, she decided. "Fleas, anyone?" Zada asked, which was answered by some serious peck-peck-pecking combined with "That flea was so yummy." "My flea was yummier." "Fleas are my favorite."

Zada deliberately didn't mention the bigger problem, which had little to do with the wind or the big cat or the fleas or even water. It had everything to do with not knowing where the moving mountain had carried Perlita and Pard, and if they could find their way to their babies.

Blowing dust can change the appearance of the landscape in disorienting ways. Even the Mission, a place both the camel and the kestrals knew well, could become hard to find. The desert was so immense, so expansive, so enormously huge, they could search and search and search and still miss each other.

Alas. Zada had to stop thinking about it. She and the chicks were safe. At least there was that. All they could do was wait. Wait for the dust to dissipate. Wait for the light to reappear. Wait. It. Out.

From their spot on the top of her head, Beulah and Wims peered through Zada's thick fur. They stretched out their necks, but in the dimness all they could see was the big absence left by their mother and father. Wims leaned sadly against his sister. "I miss Mommy and Daddy," he whimpered.

A tiny sniffle trickled from Beulah's beak. "Me t-t-t-too," she said.

Then, because when one baby cries, the other one can't help but join in, Wims burst into a mini rainstorm, so many tears they flooded Zada's furry tuft. The two peeped and hiccupped and sobbed until the whole patch was in danger of turning into a swamp. Zada had to swallow hard to keep from unleashing her own tears.

Missing. It's such a hard thing, isn't it? Zada wished she could say something that would make it all right, or just a little bit better.

It must have been a good wish because right then, in the darkness of the escarpment, dust all around, Zada could swear that she heard the faint ringing again. *Kllloookkll*. Which made her think of . . . Asiye.

*Ahh, the stories we could tell,* thought Zada. *If only . . .*

But wait. Stories?

Of course!

There were so many things Zada couldn't do. She couldn't make the wind stop blowing. She couldn't keep the air from filling up with dust. She couldn't make the light return just by asking. Worst of all, she couldn't make Perlita and Pard reappear, no matter how much she wished.

But stories. That she could do.

"Pip-pip, peepsters," Zada said, as cheerily as possible, under the circumstances. "How can I tell you about two baby camels named Zada and Asiye, with so much wailing and gnashing of beaks going on?"

There was a long moment of joint hiccupping, but at last, to Zada's relief, Beulah sucked in a big breath and wiped her face on her wing. Wims did the same, followed by a final hiccup, followed by another sniffle, followed by both of them fluffing up their new feathers and scrunching down into tiny gray-blue puff balls.

"I want to hear a st-st-story," said Beulah, in her softest voice. And in a voice even softer than that: "Me too." To which Wims added, "But make sure it's not sc-sc-scary."

"Do we have an O.O.D. (Official Okie Dokie) then?" There was no answer, but Zada was fairly

certain she could detect the baby caravanners' heads nodding up and down. "Let the saga begin," she said. And with that, she used the most time-honored beginning of all great beginnings . . . and while maybe not the most original, when you are sheltering from a massive haboob, with hopes that the local mountain lion was not in the near vicinity, who cared?

"Once upon a time . . . ," Zada began, "in a land far away . . ."

# Smyrna, Turkey

**1850**

If you could fly due north from a rocky cavern in West Texas, cross the very top of the world, soar above the Arctic ice sheets and tundra, you might catch a meltemi wind, one that rose up on a clear bright day and blasted across the frigid waters of the Black Sea. From there, you could ride on the wind's back, high above the Aegean, where you'd finally find a pier, or a dock where you could land in Smyrna, an ancient city snugged along the coast of Turkey.

Smyrna. That was where Zada's story began. There the Pasha, the man in charge of things—decreed by the sultan himself—lived in a stupendously large mansion. Legend has it that Alexander the Great once fell asleep on the mountain that overlooked the city and the bay. In his dream, an angel told him to build a palace in that very spot. Which is exactly what occurred, because when you are great, stuff happens.

We're sure that any angel flying over would be impressed. First, they'd see the imposing red dome of the mosque, which sat right in the middle of a huge walled complex. Four minarets that reached into the sky, graced the compass points—north, south, east, west. Surrounding the whole affair was a tall stone wall with round watchtowers on the corners.

Walk through the arched gate, and into the main building. Step into the large reception hall, festooned with golden candelabras and fine wood carvings, carvings of gazelle and bears and wild dogs. On one wall was a brilliant tile mosaic, featuring a forest of plane trees, their knotted trunks twisting and twining. In front of them a green-blue stream flowed by, filled with golden-scaled barbels.

Dozens of arched doorways opened into dozens of rooms, each one carpeted with finely woven rugs made from the wool of the Pasha's own flocks of white fat-tailed karaman sheep.

There was a bakery, a madrasa, an entire wing of rooms for the various members of the Pasha's family, all ringing a courtyard filled with rows of tomato plants and coriander and rich, pink Damascene roses.

Remember that mosque? First, remove shoes. Next, walk inside. Last—deep breath—look down. The blue-and-white-tiled floor gleamed in the light of a thousand candles. Look up, and there was the round ceiling of the dome, adorned with perfectly geometrical rings of floral designs and shapes. It soared into the blue ceiling of the sky.

Finally, last stop on the guided tour: at the very end of the long hallway was a large ballroom where the Pasha entertained guests from near and far, all of them bedecked in fancy outfits, rich velvet capes, billowing robes that swirled when they walked. The men wore felted fezzes and the women covered their faces with silk masks that hid their smiles, and at the same time, lit up their eyes. So much bedecking. Even the servants were bedecked.

You could say it was the posh Pasha palace.

Outside the mansion's walls, the Pasha's orchards were filled with apricots and figs and sumac. Their sweet and spicy aromas inter-twined with the salty fragrance of the sea, and altogether—sweetsy, spicy, salty—those luscious smells wafted up and down the streets. They permeated all the buildings, including—*ta-da!*— the camel nursery, which sat behind the mansion and opened onto a large field. The camel nurs-ery housed all the new mother camels and their baby calves, separate from the rest of the Pasha's larger herd.

As it turns out, the Pasha raised the finest camels in all of Anatolia (which is the old name for Turkey, but is still used even today). At any rate, we can faithfully report that between raising the figs and apricots and the elite camels, the Pasha was a highly successful governor. He was practically perfect as far as Pashas go.

Even so, more important to Zada, was Teodor, the stable master and cameleer. After her mother's, Teodor's was the first voice she ever heard. "Güzel kiz. Beautiful girl," he called her. His were the first hands to ever rub her beneath her chin, and behind her ears. He was the first to offer her a handful of juicy figs, which to this day are her favorite food *ever*. Just thinking about them made her mouth water.

Teodor. He was soft-spoken and generous and had a large mustache. When he kissed Zada on her cheek, his mustache tickled, which made her burst into her own unique camel chuckle, a combination of long, rumbly fur-covered notes, with an added *puff-puff-puff* that capped it all off.

Camel voices. Each one is different. Each one is mellifluous . . . at least to camels.

Speaking of voices . . . In those early days in the nursery barn, Zada's mama sang her baby Zada awake in the morning, and sang her to sleep at night. Such honey to Zada's baby camel ears.

There was also, in the camel nursery, a resident jerboa. He entered and exited Zada's stall through an exceptionally small hole in the corner, which was fine since he was exceptionally small, mouse-sized. He had ears that were almost as tall as his body was high, and he jumped from one side to another in zigzags that were impossible to follow, which was the point, as it kept the resident cats confused enough to throw them off his trail.

The jerboa wasn't exactly friendly, and he loved to sneak up on Zada while she was snoozing and swat at her tail. He might have had a name, but if he did, Zada couldn't tell you. All she knew was that he did a great job of snapping up the seeds scattered on the floor from her mother's dinner, a trough full of wheat and bulgur.

Zada had never seen anyone eat as fast as that jerboa. It was a wonder to behold.

But the biggest wonder of all? Zada's next stall neighbor: Asiye! She was born only a few days after Zada. She was the same coppery color, had the same rounded ears and whiskery chin. Same dark black eyes and fat toes. They were like mirror images, those two. Zada thought Asiye was the best-in-the-west. And the north, south, east, too.

Best-ever best friends. That was Zada and Asiye. The *A* to the *Z* and back again.

# The Escarpment

### 1910

All of a sudden, a stream of *StopitStopitStopit*s flew from the top of Zada's head and flat-out *stopped* Zada mid-story. Wims was in a state. He had gone from weepy to incensed in less time than it took for a jerboa to snap up a seed.

Beulah, on the other hand, was having a pout fest. Zada didn't need to see her to tell that her chin was drooping.

"Do we need an intervention?" demanded the camel.

"I just wanted to give him a lick," said Beulah. "It was an experiment to see if it tickled."

"It didn't. It was slobbery," cried Wims. "Now I have slobber on me."

"Oh dear," said Zada.

But, okay, *bird slobber*? Who knew there was such a thing? Zada had to chew on the inside of her cheek to keep from snorting.

"A LOT OF SLOBBER!" Wims shouted.

He was incensed. Put out. Piqued. Zada curled her lips together as tight as she could and squeaked, "I can see how slobber would be a problem."

Things might have gone so wrong from there, but fortunately, it seemed that Zada's squeaky voice caught the oppositionists' attention, and they momentarily forgot why they were upset. And as so often happens, when one baby bird begins to laugh, so too the other, and if their Honorary Auntie sums it all up with a stupendous belch, so much the better. Which was what happened.

But before we move on, let's just say that a rule about licking was instituted: *Keep your licks to yourself.* It was a good rule, because seriously, who wants to be covered in bird slobber?

# 12

## Smyrna, Turkey

**1850**

So, birdlings, where were we? Ahh, yes, the camel nursery. Even though it was so long ago, it was easy for Zada to revisit those early days, so full of zigzags and gambols and lullabies.

Every day Teodor checked on them. "How are the Pasha's racing camels today?" he'd ask. As it happened, both Zada and Asiye were born into the elite racing stables, a fact that made them both stand up a bit taller, hold their heads a bit higher.

Teodor told them, "As soon as you are three,

you'll be ready to try out for the Racing Corps, the Pasha's fastest camels in all of Turkey, and even beyond." He told them all about the racers in Arabia and Crimea and Egypt, and always the Pasha's camels won. Zada and Asiye could hardly wait.

"We'll be the fastest ever!" announced Zada.

Asiye agreed. "We'll fly right past those other camels."

But in the meantime, Teodor brushed them until their fur was as soft as silk. "Güzel develer," he told them. Beautiful camels. Afterward, he gave them each a handful of fat, juicy figs.

In those early days and weeks and months, the two camel calves grew quickly. In the mornings, Teodor opened their stall doors and turned them out into an open pasture filled with sweet grass. It was large enough for a dozen camels or so to have plenty of room to graze, and to the delight of Zada and Asiye, plenty of room to gallop. In the coolness of the early morning, the two friends stretched their legs and set off at a trot to the far fence, not too far away from their mothers, but a good distance for running. And run they did, their copper coats shining in the Anatolian sun.

There they'd be, munching on a bush, when something like a bolt of electricity zipped between them.

"Zada!" Asiye called out. "Let's fly!"

"Asiye!" Zada replied. "Fly, fly, fly!"

And *whoosh*! Off they went, necks stretched out, long legs reaching forward, zooming from one end of the paddock to another, zigging and zagging between the other camels. Their feet barely even touched the ground, that was how fast they went.

"Look at me," cried Zada, picking up her pace.

"Faster than a gazelle!" shouted Asiye, stretching her stride.

"Look at you," replied Zada.

"Faster than a hawk!" said Asiye.

The two continued, back and forth, round and round. Faster than fire. Faster than lightning. Faster than spit. (That last always made them chortle, and also . . . well . . . spit! Which is definitely a camel thing, and it starts early. Just saying.)

On warm summer nights, Teodor left the stall doors open so that they could enjoy the cool breezes that floated in from the Aegean Sea. In the darkness, they stood next to each other, their heads resting on each other's backs. Above them, the Camel Constellation gazed down on them.

It was led by the Camel Chief. He was easy to discern because the star that formed his eye was somewhat blue, bluer than the other stars, at any rate. Zada only had to locate that star, and she could find the rest of the caravan. Dromedaries, Bactrians, the ancient *Camelops*, the gigantic Titanotylopus. They lined up against the very ceiling of the universe, heading east, always east, as if they were walking straight into the rising sun.

While they stood there, watching the stars, Asiye said, "I have a wish."

"A wish?" said Zada.

"Yes," said Asiye. "I wish I could run so fast that the wind could lift me straight up to the sky."

"Asiye!" said Zada. "That is an excellent idea."

And then, at the same time, they said, "We could become stars!"

"The brightest stars," said Asiye. And from then on, their motto was "En parlak yildiz ol."

*Become the brightest star.*

# The Escarpment

## 1910

Zada shifted her weight. There was a fair amount of squirming coming from the denizens of the head-top habitat.

Sure enough . . . "Auntie," said Beulah, in a rather insistent voice, followed by an even more insistent chuff. "Where is Mommy?" Which was, of course, echoed by Wims. "Where is Daddy?"

*Oof*, Zada, *thinkthinkthink*. What was she supposed to say when she had nary an inkling of an idea about Perlita and Pard's whereabouts? She didn't think that telling the babies that their parents had been eaten by a gigantic mountain (which she hope hope hoped wasn't true) would be at all helpful.

But then Wims saved the day without even realizing it. He said, "I think we are hiding from them."

Hide-and-seek! Of course. And why not?

Beulah picked up on it. "We sure are good hiders, aren't we?"

"And Mommy and Daddy are good seekers," said Wims, with just the barest hint of a crack in his chirp.

"Best hiders and seekers ever," agreed Zada.

And for a reason she couldn't explain, maybe it was the simple bravery that the two babies showed, she felt like the proudest Honorary Auntie ever.

# 14

## Smyrna, Turkey

### 1851–52

Being proud reminds us of two other striplings: Zada and Asiye. Well before their humps grew out, Teodor would scratch them—the best, best scratches—with his large hands and tell them, "Someday, you will both make the Pasha proud." And then he would add, his smile as warm as honey, "And me too, my beauties."

Zada and Asiye wanted to make the Pasha proud, but more than that, they wanted to make Teodor proud. After all, Teodor took care of them.

They had never even met the Pasha. Zada wasn't sure she'd recognize him if he stood right in front of her.

"Is he short?" Zada wondered.

"He could be tall," said Asiye.

"Does he like to sing?" wondered Zada.

"Maybe."

"Or maybe not."

"It's possible."

"Does he wear a cape?" Zada asked. There was a long quiet spell between them. They absolutely knew nothing about the Pasha. But then . . .

"He might be prickly," said Asiye.

"He could be peevish," added Zada.

"What if he is the prickly peevish Pasha?" replied Zada.

Long pause . . . longer pause . . .

. . . here it comes . . .

. . . *bbllleeauurrrrrrppphhhhmomomo* (go ahead, you try to spell it), which was followed by a frenzy of gamboling.

With Teodor, it was different. Unlike with the Pasha, they knew Teodor, they knew the smell of his hands—like mint, from the mint that he added to his tea. They knew the sound of his voice, the way he hummed while he worked. And importantly, he was calm and gentle when he taught them the rules of the racers.

Most of the official regulations were handled by the jockeys, typically the younger sons from the upper-crust families, including the sons of the Pasha himself. They decided things like the location of the track, the length of the track, the number of camels in a specific race, the age groups of the camels, what color these jockey's racing clothes should be, all those technical issues. It was a lot of jockeying.

But Teodor had special rules for his special camels:

№ I: No bumping. (You'd be surprised how much camels enjoy bumping into

ONE ANOTHER. THEY'RE LIKE BUMPER CARS, ONLY CAMELS.)

№ 2: NO STICKING YOUR LEG OUT AND TRIPPING YOUR FELLOW RACERS. (YOU MIGHT ALSO BE SURPRISED TO KNOW THAT CAMELS CAN USE THEIR BACK LEGS TO KICK SIDEWAYS, ESPECIALLY IF YOU ARE, SAY, STANDING NEXT TO ONE WHO SUDDENLY DECIDES TO KICK YOU.)

№ 3: ABOVE ALL . . . NO SPITTING. (THIS JUST MEANS BEING POLITE. THAT'S ALL, REALLY.)

For the next three years, the young duo ran and ran and ran, from one end of the corral to the other, all the while growing stronger and faster.

"Let's fly," cried Asiye.

"Fly, fly, fly!" replied Zada.

And off they went, two young camels, racing each other, racing the wind.

## Mountain Lion Territory

**1910**

Zada couldn't help but notice that there was another round of fidgeting coming from the direction of her tuft.

"Hello," said Zada. "What are you two doing up there?"

Fidget. Fidget.

"Beulah?"

Fidget. Fidget. Fidget.

"Wims?"

Zada waited.

Finally Beulah said, "We're practicing our side-kicks."

And that was followed by Wims, "Yeah."

And that was followed by the inevitable, "Ouch!"

"Don't make me come up there," said Zada, which was of course impossible, because how could she climb onto her own head?

But more importantly, she realized, the sniffles seemed to have abated, at least for the moment.

Also, for the moment at least, there was still no sign of Pecos de Leon. Zada knew she had to keep her guard up, though. It was so dark beyond the cave, the wind was roaring so loud, that a mountain lion could easily slink right in. The old cat was sneaky, which was why he was old. Zada was old too, that was true. What was also true was that her memory felt as fresh as a purple sage bush after a rain.

As if they had telepathy, the chicks stopped their side-kicking and chirped into Zada's ears, a single voice in each. Stereo. "Auntie, tell us more."

"All righty, then," she said. "Hunker down."

And just as she began, a stray willy-willy slipped into the cave, made a brief appearance, then disappeared; and for the most fleeting of seconds, Zada thought she detected the faint scent of figs.

# Ephesus, Turkey

## 1853

It had been a long time since Zada had eaten figs, but her tongue still remembered the texture of their smooth skins, and the sweet honey taste of them in her mouth. Teodor always kept a handful of them in his pocket.

Mmm . . . if only . . .

But we digress.

One morning Teodor announced, "Time for a field trip." It seems that, as part of their training, Teodor wanted Zada and Asiye to practice carrying weight on their backs, as well as to strengthen their legs for distances. Endurance and strength—necessary elements for the race.

Dealing with crowds was also part of the plan. Even though Teodor had frequently led his camels through the streets of Smyrna to explore the markets and the fishing piers, those sites were not far from the nursery barn and the familiar corral.

They needed some distance training.

So Teodor strapped on their saddles and led Zada and Asiye to Ephesus, an ancient city just north of Smyrna. The Pasha's two young daughters sat astride the camels' backs.

Zada was amazed by the girls' fluty voices, and even more amazed by the open countryside. On either side of the road, there were whole fields of tulips, bursting with reds and oranges and yellows. The road itself was full of travelers, some on foot, some on donkeys, some on horses, many on camels. There were carts filled with sheep's wool and dried fish, and wagons loaded with timber and barrels of wine, some pushed, some pulled. Mile after mile, it seemed like there was something new with every step.

Several hours later, when they finally arrived at Ephesus, enormous statues, some with wings, that were more than a thousand years old, carved by the Greeks, greeted them.

Zada took one look at the giant stony figures, especially the ones with no heads, and swallowed hard. The giants loomed over them, massive. Zada started to shiver. She had never seen anyone that large . . . motionless . . . no head. Her whole being said, *Run, Zada, run!*

Meanwhile Asiye, somehow not concerned by the imposing figures, nudged Zada with her nose and said, "Don't worry. They can't see you."

Zada snorted. *Hah!* A huge ball of regurgitated wheat and bulgur rose from her three stomachs, up her neck, and . . . stand back, people.

"Zounds," said Asiye. "That was impressive!"

All at once, the statues just seemed silly. And Zada felt braver. As for the Pasha's daughters, they were aghast. Let's face it, a camel's spitball is really a mass of food that has been chewed, swallowed, chewed some more, and then steeped in gastric juices and finally launched.

With aplomb, we might add.

It could make a Pasha's princess turn a little pale.

# The Escarpment

**1910**

All the talk of wings (albeit of the marble type) must have stirred something in the breasts of our young aeronauts, because the next thing Zada heard was:

"I sure do, sure do, sure do want to fly," said Wims.

"Sure do. Me too," said Beulah.

Zada nearly said, "Well, of course you will." But in fact, she had no idea how birds learned to fly. And . . . if . . . what if . . . oh, she could hardly think of it, but if Perlita and Pard never found them . . .

well . . . what then? If the kestrels could not get liftoff, so many things could happen to them, and none of them were good.

Though falcons were like speeding arrows in the air, on terra firma they were easy bait for any number of bird-eating creatures:

bobcats,

wolves,

coyotes,

snakes,

other birds.

The list was *loooooooooooonnnnngggggg*.

Right then, Zada decided that she would make the babies stay in their penthouse apartment forever before she would let them loose in the wild. But how she could enforce that, she had no idea.

She looked out into the blowing dust. Where, oh where were Perlita and Pard? If the haboob could take out huge cottonwood trees . . . No! She was not going to go there.

The storm seemed to hear Zada's thoughts. It circled the rocky haven and let loose a chorus of howls and growls. Inside the den, the dust refused to settle down, shivering in the static air.

Beulah shivered too. Then Wims shivered. They wanted the wind to stop blowing. They wanted to go back to their nest in the cottonwood tree.

"We want our mommy and daddy," they whimpered. So much wanting.

Sniffle, sniffle, sniffle. The old camel nodded her head up and down, up and down, in a gentle rocking motion. Maybe that would help?

But rather than comforting the chicks, it only seemed to make matters worse. A whole array of hiccups and coughs rose up between Zada's ears, punctuated by a torrent of *peeppeeppeeppeep-peeppeeppeep*s.

So Zada, right then and there, made a promise she wasn't sure that she could keep.

"Someday you'll fly too, my excellent caravanners," she said, in her most comforting voice. But as soon as she said so, she could only hope for a star upon which to make a wish, because how could she make such a shaky guarantee, when there was none?

Then again, hadn't she and Asiye promised each other they would someday fly? Why, yes, yes they had.

## 18

# Smyrna, Turkey
### 1853

As it turns out, the camels were not the only animals in the Pasha's stables. There were also horses. They were smaller than the camels, and a lot more sensitive. They stamped their hooves a lot, snorted a lot, and they liked to shake their heads in ways that made their silky manes look like something the gods granted only to horses. All flowy and showy. Who does that?

Not Zada. Not Asiye.

And besides: good news, sports fans, because . . .

Halime. Naime. Rezan. Tarkan. Kahraman. Elif. Melek. The Pasha's older racers. Counting the newcomers, Zada and Asiye, there were nine, all of whom spent a good deal of time rubbing and bumping into each other. Seriously, it's a camel thing. Do not stand between camels; you might get squished.

So Zada and Asiye didn't have to pay attention at all to the snooty horses. Hah!

Even better news? Each of the nine camels came with his or her own semi-euphonic voice, which meant that whenever they lifted their heads into the air and started singing together, they created a stupefying camel chorale, the sound of which drove the horses absolutely bonkers.

What does a singing camel sound like? Well, it depends upon the camel, but the timbre and range goes from something like a low, rumbly drone, which if you were holding a glass bottle in your hand, might make it explode, to a higher-pitched *huff-huff-bbbbllllllwwaaaalll-aaaggggrrrrrllll* sort of noise, one that's impossible to truly replicate with mere letters on a page, trust me.

# 19

## Smyrna, Turkey

### 1850–56

One of Teodor's jobs as cameleer was to make and repair the saddles and bridles for both camels and horses. It was a craft he took seriously.

It wasn't long before Zada and Asiye outgrew their training halters, and it was time to create bridles worthy of their elite status. Soon they would join the older racers. Their bridles were beautiful to behold. Zada and Asiye needed equally fine bedecking.

For weeks, Teodor worked through the night, tanning leather until it was soft as cotton. Then he purchased strands of dyed lambswool—long braids of red, yellow, saffron, teal—and wove them between the cords of leather.

The last step was to adorn the ear straps with something metallic, something that would catch the glimmers from the sun.

"Gold," he said. "To make the Pasha proud."

And with that, he visited the royal metal-smith, Zafer.

The Pasha kept Zafer very busy, creating cups and saucers for his kitchens, finely etched lamps for the palace ballrooms, and tambourines for his official musicians. He made arm cuffs of gold for the Pasha's wives and silver chains for his daughters to wear around their necks. For the Pasha's sons, the smith created fine rings for their fingers and ears.

His work was of the highest quality, and the Pasha was full of gratitude. When Teodor visited Zafer and told him that he needed something special to adorn the young camels' bridles, the smith showed him an array of buttons, tassels, engraved strips, all beautiful, all worthy of the racing camels.

But Teodor wanted something even more special for his two newest racers.

Seeing the indecision on Teodor's face, Zafer knew what to do. Instead of tassels and buttons, the smith handed him a single sheet of gold.

"But what shall I do with this?" asked Teodor.

"Make something that brings you joy," said Zafer. But Teodor was dumbfounded. Joy?

"Take a walk," the metalsmith said. "And as you walk, take note of the things you love, and soon you will know what to do."

So Teodor took a walk. He noted many things.

With his eyes, he noticed the patterns that the carpet makers spun into their rugs, the way the warp and weft of the dyed threads dodged in and out and betwixt each other, making triangles and diamonds and stars.

He noticed the chirring of the pigeons, how

they billed and cooed with each other—*klllloookkll*. He also heard the high-pitched whistle of the hawks that lived in the upper stories of the local temple. *Paaaahhh paaahhh!*

He smelled the sweet aroma of dates from the palm trees and apricots and figs from the Pasha's orchards.

All these things he loved. All these things brought joy. All at once, he knew. . . .

Teodor headed straight to the paddock where Zada and Asiye were taking their midday naps, heads resting on each other's backs. "Hello, you," he said to them. He rubbed their soft, soft noses, then gave each of them a scratch beneath their chins. Finally he rubbed their rounded ears. Joy. Right at the tips of his fingers!

And just like that, the lovely ringing of the temple bells caught a ride on a warm summer breeze and wrapped itself around him. Teodor knew what he would make with the beautiful sheet of gold.

So, with the help of the metalsmith, he worked the fine metal. First he cut it into two equal pieces. Then he shaped both into small domes the size of thimbles. On the insides, he attached tiny gold clappers.

Bells!

Teodor made gold bells. One for Zada and one for Asiye. On the outsides he etched tiny palm trees, with a row of stars just above them, and a row of swirls just below to indicate the wind. With a fine-pointed stylus, he pierced the leather of each bridle, and attached the bells tightly to the straps, one that held fast just below Zada's left ear and the other next to Asiye's right ear.

Perhaps the metal con-tained a spell, because indi-vidually neither bell had much of a ring. But when the two camels stood side by side, it was as if the bells discovered their voices and sang right out loud, in a clear, chiming echo, rather like the *kllloookkll* of the stable pigeons.

If you didn't know it was the bells that made that sound together, you might think it was the pigeons after all. Or perhaps the distant sound of a flute, a piper's welcome to the evening stars. Above all, it seemed like the sound of their ringing created a circle of happiness in every chiming note.

When Teodor gave the two friends the bells, he said this: "May these bells bring joy."

Where there is one, there is the other.

# Somewhere

**1910**

There are other things that go together. Salt and pepper. Thunder and lightning. Twists and turns. Perlita and Pard.

From their very first meeting, they had rarely left each other's sides, and even then, only for short forays to gather food for the babies. No more than ten minutes or so at best. And though Pard would be the first to admit that Perlita was prone to fits of drama, he couldn't imagine being away from her for longer than the previously mentioned ten minutes.

She was his true love. And he was hers. They were each other's one and onlys.

But when the haboob grabbed them, it pushed them in separate directions. Pard was in a panic. His frantic voice filled the roiling air with his loudest *klee*s and *killy*s, hoping they'd break through the horrible roar of the wind. Like the point on an arrow, he aimed his beak and flew directly into the tempest, but no matter how hard he flapped, he could not make any headway. Instead, he just kept getting tossed and tumbled.

At last, exhausted, he realized that he needed to find some sort of shelter until the wind died down. Somehow, he discovered a sturdy creosote bush, leaning over so far it was practically pressed into the sand, but miraculously still rooted to the desert floor. It wasn't perfect, but it would do. Pard burrowed against its twisty limbs, wrapped himself as tightly as he could with his battered wings, and tucked his head beneath his shoulder. His heart thrummed in his ears.

As if it wasn't bad enough that he couldn't find Perlita, he had no idea where his babies were either. Wims and Beulah. "Dear Zada," he whispered, his throat raspy from calling for Perlita. "Be safe." It was a wish he made with all his might.

**21**

## The Escarpment

**1910**

Zada took a long, deep breath. Luckily, her camel nostrils did an excellent job of filtering out the dust. The storm outside continued its near-constant roar. It showed no signs of stopping. None.

How long before their luck ran out, she wondered, before Pecos de Leon made what she knew would be his inevitable appearance? As soon as the wind died down, they would have to make a break for the Mission. No question.

She could hear Wims and Beulah peck-peck-

pecking between her ears. For the first time ever, she was grateful for sand fleas.

There were so many things she couldn't control—the wind, the stars, the not-knowing of what had happened to Perlita and Pard.

*Ooof!* She felt an ache, right in her very center. If only she had awakened earlier. If only she had been quicker to get to her feet. If only she had recognized the storm for what it was, maybe . . .

But the hard truth was, she didn't do any of those, and now . . . Perlita and Pard had vanished, and all Zada could do about it was wish with all her might: "Be safe."

**22**

*Anywhere*

What we can say about the wind is that it is.

Neither young nor old, it comes, it goes. The
same wind that crept around the massive feet of
the dinosaurs now swirls around the toes of baby
koalas.

It's not like trees that grow old, or candles that
flame out with time.

That breeze that looped around Zada once
circled the giant *Camelops* of ancient Texas. It loops
around you, it loops around me. It knew our grand-

mothers and our great-grandmothers and our great-times-a-thousand grandmothers.

It knew Zada's ancestors too, even her pre-historic grandmother, *poebrotherium,* who was smaller than a coyote.

The wind. It just is.

**23**

# Smyrna, Turkey

**1853–54**

Zada's mother had told her all about her ancestors: the warrior camels of the sultanate; the trekking camels in the Sudan; the dairy camels of Tripoli; the famous fleet of racing camels in Arabia.

There were Zada's grandmothers and grandfathers, her aunts and uncles, her cousins and second cousins and third cousins and cousins galore. And they were all renowned for feats of endurance, including crossing the Alps with Hannibal and traversing the ice bridges with the woolly mammoths.

The camels in Zada's family were always the first choice for the merchants who traveled the Silk Road on their quests for exotic spices and finely woven fabrics.

Importantly, the Pasha not only bred his camels for racing, but he also bred camels for the great armies of the world. For centuries camels were used to carry warriors and weapons, the materiel for battle. And no camels were braver than those raised by the Pasha. Commanders from Rome and generals from Crimea and admirals in the Ukraine, all sought the Pasha's camels for their willingness to fight with courage and heart.

As for Zada and Asiye, they were bred for the race. Only the most elite of the Pasha's camels were chosen for the track. It was as if they had the very wind itself in their legs. They were anxious to begin their training.

As soon as they turned three, they knew . . . it was time. For their whole young lives, they had dreamed of the track, especially the races at the

Pasha's annual festival, which he held in honor of his birthday.

There would be merchants selling hand-dyed scarves and spicy peppers, dancers spinning on their toes, magicians casting love spells for forlorn sailors, and finally, the biggest event, the camel races. It was the richest camel race in the world. The Pasha could afford to offer the highest prize because nobody ever beat his camels. So the treasure went right back into his coffers.

Nevertheless, the prize was a lure, an incentive for the other camel barons. The best racing camels, from the best stables in the world, would compete. There would be racing camels from all across the region, from the hills of Greece, from the shores of Egypt and Spain, from the lowlands of Persia. All of them wanted only one thing: to beat the Pasha's camels and claim the grand prize.

Zada and Asiye couldn't wait for their turn to show how fast they were. So on the cusp of their third birthdays, Teodor announced, "It's time, my beauties." The two friends held their heads up high as Teodor led them to the practice track. They were nervous, but they were ready.

"So ready," said Zada.

"Very ready," said Asiye.

"Extremely ready," they said together.

The older camels nodded from the paddock as the two passed by. "Good luck," they called. It was a day of anticipation and most of all, speed! Everyone lined up to watch the two new racers, the ones they had seen flying around the corral. It was their time to shine.

Teodor patted their noses. "Güzel develer," he told the pair. Then he lifted their training saddles atop their backs and strapped them on.

"Ready," said Zada.

"More than ready," said Asiye.

"Stupendously ready," they said together, two ready camels and their cameleer. Teodor led them down the central road, past the markets, past the fez factory, all the way to a long strip of sandy beach, which served as the practice track.

The identical bells on their harnesses chimed, *klllooookkll.* Above their heads, a noisy crew of seagulls called, "Are you ready?"

"Ready," answered the camels. The day was bright and cool. The sand was warm beneath their toes. Everything was perfect.

"Time to fly," they said together, bumping against each other.

Teodor led them to the farthest end of the beach, which he used as a starting line. "All the way down and back," he told them. Finally he gave them one last pat and released their leads. But when he gave them the whistle . . .

Zada froze.

She could not take a single step.

She could not even put a toe over that line.

There was no get up, no go, nothing.

Asiye too. She stretched out her long neck and . . . well . . .

Fear wrapped its arms around the two and squeezed.

"What if . . . ," asked Zada.

". . . we *lost!*" exclaimed Asiye.

"What if we are the very first camels to cause the Pasha to lose his grand prize?" The Pasha was known far and wide for his kindness, but it was easy to be kind when you never, ever lost anything. Would losing his big prize make him less kind?

"What would happen?" asked Asiye. "What would he do?"

"Would he s-s-sell us to a traveling circus?" stammered Zada. "Turn us into camel stew?"

Worst of all . . . "What if we have to become *pack* camels?" (Which all camels know are the lowest of the camel ranks. How would they ever get past the shame?)

For decades, the Pasha's camels had *always* come in first place, always won, never *ever ever ever* lost.

But . . .

What if . . .

I mean . . . it could happen . . .

Zada couldn't budge. Asiye, too, was stuck in her tracks. They were so paralyzed by the bevy of what-ifs that they couldn't even feel their toes.

Thank goodness for Teodor. He rubbed their long necks and scratched the soft fur beneath their chins. He told them how proud he was of them. Another cameleer might have swung a heavy cane across their hindquarters. Some other trainer might have pierced their noses and jabbed a pointed wooden stick through them, and then tugged on them, the pain forcing the camels to move. Anyone besides Teodor might have cursed his camels and told them that they were worthless.

But none of those cameleers were Teodor. He simply stood beside them and waited. And soon all that patience and kindness worked. The fear that held them in its arms let go.

Asiye leaned over and whispered into Zada's ear, "En parlak yildiz ol!"

It was all they needed. Teodor blew his whistle again. The two friends held their heads up, stretched out their long necks, and off they flew along the water's edge. In that first practice race, they became who they were meant to be: members of the Pasha's elite racing team. So fast that if you blinked, you might not even see them.

For the next three years, not a single camel could outrace them. Sometimes Zada won by a nose. Other times Asiye won. But just as often, they tied. And the Pasha's grand prize was safe.

**24**

# The Escarpment

## 1910

Despite the rumble of the wind as it passed, for a fleeting moment, a small sliver of happy worked its way into Zada's mind. Memories have that power. But happy is hard to hold on to when a ruckus erupts between your ears. A cacophony of *klee*s and *killy*s, chirps and peeps. In short, a perturbation.

Beulah piped up first. "Wims put his toe in my face."

"But she poked me with her beak, right on my head," retorted Wims.

"Did not," said Beulah.

"Did too," said Wims.

"Not not not," said Beulah.

"Ouch! She pecked my head again!"

*Peeppeeppeeppeeppeeppeeppeeppeeppeep-peeppeeppeep!*

Zada's nerves began to jangle. It might have been a good time to spit, but how could she spit on her own head?

"Your toe stinks!" screeched Beulah.

"No more pecking!" chirped Wims.

"Ouch! Get your ugly toe away from me!"

"Quit pecking!"

Finally Zada's composure cracked. "ENOUGH ALREADY!"

It was such a loud holler that she thought she might have blown a hole in the dusty air, because all of a sudden, a stray beam of light crept into the cave. True, it was a tentative beam of light. But as reticent as it was, it seemed to have cracked something open. Something like an eerie silence.

The threesome held their collective breath. Then . . .

"Auntie!" said Wims. "You made the storm stop!" Sure enough, the steady whistle that had engulfed them for the past few hours disappeared. The wind died down, leaving trillions of particles of sand and dust wafting in the air. And wafting is not swirling. Wafting is *less* storm. And much less noise.

In fact, the quiet was so loud that it seemed to inspire the babies to give their argument a rest. And thank goodness for that.

But Zada thank-goodnessed too soon, because the cessation of quarreling immediately turned into a round of chuffs and puffs, followed by no small number of *hhmpphs*, which were, let's face it, not at all amusing to Zada.

"Do we need a lesson in sportsmanlike behavior?" she asked.

Zada leaned a bit to the left. Her head ached. Her ears ached. But especially, her *knees* ached.

If not for the wily Pecos, she would have lowered herself onto the ground and given them a much-needed rest. But it was too risky. If the lion showed up, she would never be able to get up in time to escape his probable pounce.

And therein rose another unanswerable question: Would Zada's knees hold out until she could reach the Mission? It was still a long walk away from the escarpment.

Then, as if to reassure them, she sent thought beams to her knees. *Just a few more miles. Just a few.*

And sensing an opening between all the chicks' chuffs, puffs, and *hhmmphs*, because let's admit it, they couldn't last forever, Zada asked, "Are we ready to hear about the fairy chimneys?"

In a burst of enthusiasm, Beulah popped out of the tuft, hopped onto the top of Zada's right ear, stretched her fluffy body, and flapped her not-ready-for-flight-yet wings. "Ready," she said.

"Me too," said Wims, flapping his own wings, but

still not leaving the tuft. No matter. The wing flapping sounded like an O.O.D. (Official Okie Dokie) if she'd ever heard one. She felt herself relax. Just a little bit.

Sometimes, it seems, the storyteller needs the story as much as the listeners, and after all, there was so much more to tell.

# 25

# Cappadocia

## 1855 OR SO

If you mix the wind with water in all its forms—liquid, gas, ice—the combination can do a number on the landscape. Take Cappadocia, for example.

There came a day when the Pasha was invited to bring his racing camels for a tournament just outside the town of Cappadocia. It was part of a larger festival that happened only every few years. Camels from all over Anatolia and Asia, including the famed Bactrians from distant Mongolia, would be there. So of course, the Pasha announced, "Field trip!"

"I love field trips," said Zada.

"Me too," said Asiye. And with that, she broke into her own unique camel song. Which in turn made Zada raise her voice, and that made the other camels chime in. It was hallelujah all around, only in Camel, which becomes . . . wait for it . . . *camelujah!*

Oh, bird-kateers, in case we haven't told you by now, the major thing about Asiye? She had a knack for finding happy in everything, and when she did, a chorus was sure to follow.

So, off they went to Cappadocia. Teodor tied them together in a caravan, and they hit the trail. As they walked, Teodor chanted their names: *Asiye, Halime, Naime, Rezan, Tarkan, Kahraman, Elif, Melek, and Zada.*

Unlike their trip to Ephesus, which took only a few hours, getting to Cappadocia took several long days, and many more on top of them.

But it was worth it, because as they approached, there, right in the middle of nowhere, rose an outcropping of fairy chimneys. Not wee, tiny fairy abodes. No, these were gigantic, with multiple rooms carved into them, including a church.

All carved by wind and snow and running water, over millions of years.

"Enchanting," said Asiye. "I can almost smell the fairies."

Which . . . what?

Because seriously? What does a fairy even smell like? Another thing about Asiye, Zada now realized, was that she saw or smelled—the world in surprising ways. And that made everything seem brand-new.

And did they win their races?

Did they make the Pasha proud?

Do we even need to answer those questions?

# 26

# Smyrna, Turkey and All over Texas

Have we told you that Teodor wore a turban? Of course, lots of folk wore turbans. To Zada and Asiye, Teodor's turban reminded them of the tulips that grew in their native country. Tulips growing wild. Tulips growing tame. Red tulips streaked with yellow. Yellow tulips streaked with red.

Teodor's turban was none of those colors. Rather, it was bright white, to help reflect the desert sun and keep him cool. Whenever the camels noticed his turban, they thought, *Teodor has a tulip on his head.*

Tulips made absolutely no difference to the wind. Nor did turbans. Tulips. Turbans. Pansies. Porkpies. Dahlias. Derbies. Buttercups. Bowlers. The wind gets a kick out of tossing them all about.

Same with the boats at sea . . .

**27**

# Smyrna, Turkey

**1856**

One day an envoy from the United States Army caught a group of westerlies and sailed into the Mediterranean Sea, where they docked in Tunisia. There the captain began a search for a coterie of camels to take back to their country, a fairly new country on the opposite side of the world.

The captain and the crew managed to purchase a few camels in Tunis and a few more in Crimea; they bought up five camels here, and three camels there, loaded all of them on the ship, and made their way to Smyrna, where they approached the Pasha with an offer to buy a number of his very best camels.

Of course, the Pasha was extremely pleased. How wonderful it would be to send his finest camels to the new country across the sea. His camels would be excellent representatives of the Pasha's prowess as the leading camel broker in the world. He made a declaration: "It's an honor of the highest sort to sell some of my very best camels to the army of the United States of America."

And then he called for Teodor to bring forward his nine finest camels. Of course, Teodor chose his favorites: Asiye, Halime, Naime, Rezan, Tarkan, Kahraman, Elif, Melek, and Zada. He led the nine to the west portico of the Pasha's enormous house. The officers from the United States watched as the camels, their coats aglow in the setting sun, passed by for inspection. They all agreed: these were the finest camels they'd seen.

And then the Pasha, in a rare moment of largess, made a decision. Instead of *selling* his top nine camels, he decided to present them as a gift. Imagine being a gift. Not a gift like a puppy or a miniature goat. Those are companion animals, mostly. No. Zada and Asiye and the other seven were gifts of honor, of national pride. And to make the gift even better, he arranged to send Teodor with them, to teach the Americans how to manage a caravan.

The night before they left, the Pasha held a majestic celebration. He invited all the townspeople to attend, opening the gates of his palace to anyone who wished to come. Inside there were tables filled with plates of spicy pide and dolma, followed by platters of baklava cut into bite-sized pieces. There were pots of boza and red-leafed tea and Turkish coffee and camel's milk for drinking.

The sounds of musicians' instruments ricocheted off the walls—the rattle of the tambourine, the strumming of the kanuns and saz, the kaval with its fluty tones—all blended together into a happy mixture of festivity and cheer. The dancers spun so fast it seemed they might pirouette right through the vast hand-painted ceiling of the Pasha's mansion.

Then, the next day, Zada and Asiye, and their stablemates, plus Teodor, joined twenty-five other camels aboard the USS *Supply*, a ship that originally carried staples for the US Navy, but had been carefully recommissioned to carry camels. Some of the other camels already on board came from Kashmir, some came from Egypt, more came from Arabia, and there were two that came from the wildest regions of Mongolia: Bactrians, the kind with two humps instead of one. Together, they would, all thirty-four, be the first of their species to set foot in Texas since the last dwindling years of the Pleistocene.

# The Escarpment

## 1910

Outside the mountain lion's lair, the wind resumed its gale forces. Wind does that. It blows and blows and blows, fast, fast, faster. Then, from out of the blue, it pauses, takes a deep breath; it leaves a billion particles of dust hanging in the air, caught in the barely-there sunlight, all glimmery.

Just as Zada caught her own breath, she sensed that the wind wasn't as loud as before. In fact, it was barely there. Hardly any howling to be heard. Nary a whisper. Nary a moan. Nary a *pppfffffttttthhh*.

But then, "AUNTIE, IT'S DARK IN HERE," came from deep inside her right ear, followed by "LOOK, I FOUND MY OWN CAVE," coming from her left ear.

It seems Wims had tunneled his way into Zada's left ear, and Beulah had done the same in Zada's right ear. Ear-birds!

"Okay, then," said Zada, "but please don't—" Before she could finish, sure enough: *PEEEEPPP-PEEEEEPPPPEEEEEPPPPP!* Which made Zada's eyes water.

"Ooof!" She resisted the urge to flick her head, which would send both babies flying (and not in a good way). But then Wims asked, "AUNTIE, WHAT HAPPENED NEXT?"

"Well," she said, hoping like crazy they would make their ways out of her ears. "There was a ship. . . ."

## 29

## Atlantic Ocean

### 1856

The *Supply* belonged to the US Navy, whose home port was in New York Harbor. It had sailed all over the world, including around the very tip of the American continent, and across the Pacific Ocean to Japan and back. It had traveled the seven seas, one sea after another, and always it carried supplies for the navy, supplies like water and oats and rum and ropes and tackles and extra sheeting for torn sails. Supplies like that.

But when

the army decided to buy camels for an experiment, the ship was refitted and made into a sailing camel stable. Just below the main deck, the camels were placed in individual stalls, built especially for them, with straps that would hold them safe when the seas were rough.

The straps had been ingeniously designed by a lieutenant named Porter. They helped keep the camels from being tossed about and injured when the waves were high and the wind blew wild.

Maybe Lieutenant Porter was clairvoyant, because only days after Zada and Asiye and the other camels were loaded onto the boat, before they were even out of the Mediterranean, they ran into some of the worst weather that the *Supply* had ever encountered.

"Batten down the camels!" cried Lieutenant Porter. Whereupon the sailors lined the stalls with extra hay and urged the camels to lower themselves into it, then strapped them down.

There they were, thirty-four camels, animals

who had spent their whole lives in the sun, all stowed belowdecks in a space that had no light at all, but for a couple of flickering whale-oil lanterns. Imagine those camels, creatures who spent their days gamboling beneath cloudless skies, being strapped to the floor so that their knees were folded underneath them, unable to even stand and stretch. The straps cut into Zada's thick fur. They rubbed against her back and neck and sides, trapped her and her sailing mates. She raised her head and bawled. And bawled. And bawled.

Teodor could not console her, even though he rubbed her face and checked that the straps were secure.

Imagine the unfamiliar odors—whale oil and wet hay and dried fish. All those strange smells, all mixed together, making Zada's stomachs churn.

And all the while, the boat rose and fell, rising atop the waves and dropping into the valleys between them, landing with a crash, the wind braying like an angry sea monster come to gobble them all up. (Like the haboob, but wet.)

Day after night after day after night, and longer, the *Supply* fell victim to the vicious whims of the ocean. Finally, worn out from so much bawling, her throat as dry as gravel, Zada tucked her head beside her folded legs and tried to hold herself together. The boat leaned so far to the right that had she not been tied down, she would have toppled against its wooden sides. The hated straps were the only thing that kept her from being thrown through the air. Then, as soon as the ship righted itself, it leaned to the left.

The straps held. The flickering lantern flickered out, leaving only shadows; the howling wind slipped through the ship's timbers. Ice-cold water seeped through the decks above and soaked into her fur. She could not stop shivering.

Night after day after night after day. Zada lost track of time. Dizziness enveloped her; at last it spun her into a weary sleep, a sleep so heavy she could barely remember what it felt like to be awake.

But then in the dark, somehow above the howl of the gale, Zada heard the familiar *kllloookkll*.

Asiye!

Next thing she knew, Asiye's voice found her ear and settled there: "Zada," she said. "I think we're flying." She said it just as the boat rose into the sky in a nearly vertical pitch, hovered for a full ten or twelve seconds, then zoomed into a deep trough.

And just like that, the dark didn't seem quite so dark anymore.

# The Escarpment

**1910**

Zada thought she heard something that sounded like a sentence. She listened again.

Yep. There it was.

Wims, having thankfully stepped out of her left ear, said, in a voice full of serious, "Auntie, camels don't fly."

Then Beulah, who had also exited Zada's other ear, added, "Camels don't have wings."

"Yeah," said Wims. "No wings."

"This is true," said Zada. "But maybe there are other ways to fly."

# Atlantic Ocean

**1856**

Camels are designed for open spaces. Give them a mountain and they'll climb it. Give them a desert and they'll cross it. Give them a long route and they'll cover every inch and then some. They need the daylight and the starshine and the *pah-pah-pah* of hawks riding the thermals.

Zada needed all of the above. For the long journey across the sea, three months to be exact, she stayed in her stall aboard the *Supply*. When the waves were calm, Teodor unfastened the hated straps and allowed her to stand up and move around. But when the seas were rough, she was forced to withstand the straps again.

Her only comfort was knowing that Asiye was nearby. Even though she couldn't see her, she could hear her calling out. And of course, there were the bells, the ones that Teodor had created just for them, fastened to their bridles.

*Kllllooookkll.*

The bells chimed and chimed. It was as if the camels had their own language. And in that shared language, the two friends dreamed of birds and the sweetness of dates and the blue eye of the Chief Camel, the constellation that led the starry camel caravan.

Finally there came a quiet morning, a morning when the sailors threw open the porthole windows and let the breeze and daylight come rushing in. All that fresh air and fresh light poured onto the camel deck.

Zada felt her heart rise, and in the midst of all that freshness, she heard Teodor say a new word.

"Texas." It seemed that Texas was the land that they were headed toward. And sure enough, on a May day in 1856, Zada, Asiye, and the other camels sailed into Matagorda Bay, to a deep-water port called Indianola. And even though it wasn't the same as her birthplace, when Zada finally stepped ashore, after so many months in a dark, wet stall, she thought it might be the most beautiful spot on the planet. She thought it might be something like paradise.

**32**

# The Escarpment

## 1910

This dark den, with its opening that looked like a behemoth mouth, was decidedly not paradise. Though Zada was doing her best to stay calm for the chicks, her steadiness was dwindling.

For one thing, though she knew that the sand fleas would be enough for the chicks in the immediate here and now, soon they would need water. But the dust-filled air outside the cave was still too suffocating to venture to the Mission. With luck, there would be water there. With more luck, there would be Pard and Perlita, waiting for them.

But for another thing—and this was a more pressing question, the question that made her teeth hurt—where was Pecos de Leon? It seemed like a flat-out miracle that she had seen neither hide nor hair of the mountain lion.

And for a third— Gah! A raucous *peeppeep-peeppeeppeeppeeppeeppeep!* broke out between her ears. It was so rowdy it made her eyebrows arch.

"Hey now, hey now," she soothed. "What is the problem?"

"There was a t-t-t-tick," stammered Wims. "And Beulah ate it."

Beulah protested, "It was the most delicious tick ever."

"B-b-b-but I found it," said Wims.

"You are a good tick finder," said Beulah.

"But it was mmmiiiiinnne," he fumed.

"And it was sooooo yummy," said Beulah.

Which launched them into an amazing bally-
hoo of *klee*s and *killy*s and *peeppeeppeeppeep-
peeppeeppeeppeep*s.

Then, midst the fury, Zada felt tiny, spiky
pokes, like cactus spines, piercing her head. It
was Wims standing on the very ends of his toes
and hopping like mad (he was *hopping mad*), and
in a split second of ultimate pique—*oof!*

Followed by . . .

*OH NO! OH NO! OH NO!*

Zada gasped. This could not be happening.
But yes. This was happening: Beulah, in all her
baby glory, was sliding-sliding-sliding, all the
way from Zada's head, down her neck.

"Oh no, oh no, oh no," Wims cried. "I didn't
mean it!"

*Oh no! Oh no! Oh no!* Zada thought. Beulah
couldn't fall, she couldn't. Zada would never be
able to get her back up again.

Faster than she'd moved in ten . . . no . . . twenty
years, Zada dropped to her knees and stretched

out her neck. Out, out, out, as if reaching for the finish line in one of the Pasha's races, and . . .

. . . the slip-sliding *sssssllllloooowwweddd* . . .

And . . . stopped.

Everyone sucked in a breath.

Hold it. Hold it.

At last, from the direction of Beulah's beak, came a very thin *peep*.

There was a collective exhale.

Then, in her ever-so-calmest voice, Zada gently coaxed Beulah to scooch up her neck, which she was holding so flat that she was getting a neck cramp. "Easy . . . that's the way . . . just a little farther . . ." and bit by bit, scooch by scooch, Beulah finally made her way back to the safety zone atop Zada's head. *Whew!*

Wims, a penitent passel of remorse and relief, flung himself at his sister. "I'm so sorry. I didn't mean it," he cried over and over and over. Which was okay with Beulah for approximately one half of one second. Squirming out of his embrace and resisting a huge urge to lick him, she stood on her toes and stretched to her highest height of approximately five inches and furiously flapped her wings. Then she glared at him and declared, "That tick was soooooo delicious!"

Zada considered plucking all their feathers, but right then, there was a bigger problem in the cave: she needed to get back up, because . . . hello . . . mountain lion! It was only a matter of time now. She knew this.

But she also knew that she needed a moment. It would take every ounce of her energy to stand back up. Her quick descent to the ground had jarred her already shaky knees.

*Think, Zada. Think, think, think.*

But thinking reminded her that despite the happy outcome, Beulah's slide was too close. It could so easily have gone so terribly wrong. And if it had, what then? How would she ever be able to face Perlita? Or Pard?

They had entrusted their best beloved babies,

their Wims and Beulah, the most important, utterly valuable, profoundly treasured parts of their hearts to her, Honorary Auntie. Perlita and Pard hadn't even hesitated. And what had Zada done? She had taken them right into the lair of a notorious mountain lion. That was what she had done.

*Oof!* A wave of panic rose up from her bellies. She closed her eyes.

She had to get back on her feet, and once there, she had to make sure that the babies stayed put, so as soon as the wind died down, they could make a run for it.

But the wind wasn't having it. A huge gust blasted against the outer walls and roared as it blew by. *Not yet,* it seemed to say. *Not yet.*

Miraculously, and who can even explain why? Maybe the growling wind? Or maybe bickering just eventually gets old. Whatever the reason, the chicks stopped their incessant back-and-forth and scrunched down into her fur. Beulah spoke up. "Auntie?" she asked. "Tell us more about the caravan."

Wims chimed in, "I want to hear more about the caravan too."

"Me first," said Beulah. "I want to hear about it first."

"No, me first," said Wims.

*Ahh,* thought Zada. Perhaps telling more of the story would buy her some time to recover, enough so that she could get back on her feet.

"I will tell you at the same time," said Zada. And because the wind loves a good story as much as anyone, an invisible willy-willy slipped through the opening, curled up at her feet, and settled into the floor of the cave.

"The caravan," she said. "Well . . ."

**33**

# Indianola, Texas

**1856**

The camels were so happy to get off that boat, they couldn't help themselves. As soon as they stepped onto the beach, they gamboled. In the annals of camels, there had never been so much bumping and side-kicking and back-kicking and front-kicking. All of that was mixed in with the camel chorus, an assortment of hollers and gurgles and growls and rumbles and huffs and puffs and *bbbbuuuuwww-hhhhhaaaaalllls*.

All the horses from the town went on high alert. Those Texas steeds had obviously never seen camels before.

The combination of hollering and gamboling set the resident equines into a frenzy of bucking and snorting. They reared up onto their hind feet, kicked each other, even cracked a bunch of teeth and jawbones. That was followed by an even bigger round of mane shaking and tail flicking. *Always with the manes.* Horses. So sensitive.

Anyways, despite the hullabaloo from the horses, the US Army leased out a property just outside the town that had a large barn and a big paddock. It seemed a perfect place to quarter the camels. However, a strategic mistake was made when it came to fencing.

Someone decided that the best fencing material for keeping the camels penned up inside the property—as well as for keeping other critters out—would be a high wall of prickly pear cactus. After all, it grew fast and thick. It was extremely prickly. And it worked well for penning in horses, mules, hogs, sheep, and other farm types. It should work for camels, too.

But what the camels saw when they noticed the fence wasn't *fence*. It was *dinner!* In less time than it takes to say "jumping jackrabbit," those camels mowed the prickly pear down to tiny nubs. They set a land record for the dispatching of a fence. Which meant that fairly soon there were camels roaming the city streets of Indianola and wreaking all sorts of havoc: eating shrubs, stomping on front porches, taunting the horses.

Pretty quickly, the townsfolk of Indianola objected. In fact, they objected mightily. So the army packed up and marched their camel herd to a better place. Just a bit northwest of San Antonio, they arrived in a spot known as Camp Verde. It had better fencing than Indianola, and the horses didn't seem so edgy. All in all, a good move.

Not a single camel in the herd missed Indianola.

"Good riddance," said Zada.

"So long," said Asiye.

What the two did miss, however, was running. They were, after all, among the Pasha's most elite racing camels. Right up until the moment that she boarded the *Supply*, Zada had run practically every day of her life. Even gamboling was not the same as stretching her long neck and legs forward and taking off.

"Faster than a zooming arrow," said Asiye.

"Faster than a blaze of lightning," said Zada.

"Faster than a spitball," said Asiye. Which of course, made her start singing, and that set off a camel chorale in the corral. It was a happy moment in the camel lot.

As the days passed, Zada kept waiting for Teodor to lead them to the track, but that day never came. Instead, one morning he strapped a different kind of saddle on their backs. Not a lightweight racing saddle. Rather, it was a special kind of contraption for carrying supplies. He tightened it and filled it all up with hay, pounds and pounds of hay. To Zada's utter dismay, it seemed that she and Asiye, along with the rest of the herd, were going to be used as *pack* animals, the very lowest of the camel ranks.

Shame. It was an even heavier burden than the supplies that were strapped to her back. Zada was beside herself with humiliation. At once, she folded first her front legs and then her back legs, and lowered herself onto the ground. How could she, one of the Pasha's fastest camels, find herself in such a terrible position?

"What is this?" asked Asiye, just as disgruntled as Zada.

But then Teodor leaned against Zada's side. He leaned against Asiye's side. He rubbed their long necks and kissed their cheeks. "Güzel develer," he said. "Remember, you are representing the Pasha. You are gifts." Then he told them how happy the Pasha would be to see his royal camels help lay out a new route from the east to the west of the brand-new United States of America.

It seemed that Zada and Asiye and the rest of the herd would make a long trek from Texas to San Diego, to survey a new route for the railroad.

"Gurur duymalisiniz," he told them. "You'll be making history."

Zada didn't really care about making history, especially as a pack camel. But she did want to make the Pasha proud. Beside her, Asiye said, "Field trip!" And well, when your best friend puts it that way . . . But first, Zada brought up, from the depths of her stomachs, an enormous belch.

"That was impressive," said Asiye. And despite the humiliation of the packs, they both stood up.

Zada couldn't help it. She smiled. The bells that Teodor had made for them chimed together in their ears. *Kllloookkll*. Just like that, the first official trek of the United States Army Camels commenced.

Unlike the mules and horses, the camels were

way less water-consuming. Point them in the direction of a tasty cactus or shrub, and bingo! In fact, some of the caravan camels actually carried barrels of water and bales of hay for the aforementioned mules and horses.

"They're so needy," said Asiye. Of course, she was speaking of the horses. Zada replied, "Yes, they are." But she had to admit to a certain fondness for the mules. She never spied them shaking their heads or manes—not even once.

# 34

## Camp Verde, Fort Tejon, and . . .

### 1857–67

It didn't take long for the camels to prove their worth. The caravan, with Teodor leading them,

successfully traversed the western half of the continent not once, but any number of times. To and fro they went, step by careful step.

Even though they missed racing, the camels loved being on the trail. There was so much to see:

Bison in the thousands. And more thousands.

Scorpions (not friendly).

Rattlesnakes (also not friendly).

Pack rats, which Asiye declared as useless, because they were way too small to pack anything, unlike herself and Zada.

Saguaro cacti, so tall they seemed to touch the sky.

Armadillos, who looked like four-footed Conquistadors. All that armor.

Horned toads. They could puff up to twice their size and squirt blood from their eyes. Seriously.

Longhorn cattle. More to come about them.

Joshua trees and golden hawks and chuck-wallas.

At almost every stop, they met new people: Cherokees. Lipan Apaches. Tonkawa. Chumash. People whose families had lived there for centuries, whose long-ago ancestors lived beside Zada's long-ago ancestors, those giant Titanotylopus who migrated over the very top of the world, across the frozen tundra and into Europe and Asia.

As we've said, camels are excellent trekkers. They've been doing it since the dawn of time.

# Southwestern Territories
# North America

**1858–63**

From Camp Verde to Fort Tejon and back again the caravan went. And each journey took them on a different route.

Sometimes they marched for twenty miles in a day, or more. Often the caravan traveled in the early morning hours, rested during the heat of the day, and then, just as the sun set, traveled for a while longer.

When night fell, the soldiers built a bonfire and the camels folded themselves onto the ground and watched the sparks fly into the cold night air. Sometimes, one of the soldiers strummed a guitar or played a fiddle or squeezed a concertina and sang right out loud. It didn't sound at all like the music of the Pasha's court, with its tambourines and kanuns, but it wasn't horrible.

Truth was, Zada and Asiye preferred the tunes of the distant song dogs, which always seemed to accompany them, regardless of the territory. Even though they only rarely saw one, they knew the dogs were nearby.

As if the stars agreed, straight over their heads marched the Camel Caravan, led by the Camel Chief. Even on nights when the sky was so full of moonlight it felt like day, Zada could still see his gleaming blue eye.

**36**

# Somewhere

**1910**

American kestrels might be small, but they are full of grit. And at that particular moment, *grit* was the operative word. In fact, Perlita was so full of it that she was sure she had doubled in size. All sixteen cubic inches of her were coated in a thick layer of West Texas grit.

The haboob had first lifted Perlita higher into the sky than she had ever flown, then carried her aloft for what seemed like hours. How far it had swept her from her nest in the cottonwood, she couldn't tell. When the storm had finally released her from its windy fist, she had dropped like a stone, laden as she was with grit.

Fortunately, mercy stepped in at the exact right moment. Instead of landing on the hard ground, where Perlita would most definitely have gone *poof* for the second time in one day, she fell right into a massive tumbleweed, which wrapped her in its branches like a cage. Trapped!

Then, unfortunately, the tumbleweed did what tumbleweeds do—it tumbled. Across the landscape, through the arroyos, over the ridges, it carried Perlita. Bumpity-bumpity-bumpity. Ouch ouch ouch!

Up. Down. Sideways. The tumbleweed spun its captive every which way.

How could she tell whether it was carrying her farther and farther from Wims and Beulah, or closer and closer?

"Stupid tumbleweed!" she tried to say. Only, thanks to a mouthful of . . . you know . . . grit! . . .

it came out more like, "Ttthhhuuppdd thummblll-wuud." Nothing, *not one blessed thing*, looked familiar to her, not even her own toes, which were above her head, which was not where her toes were meant to be.

And where, she thought, exactly *where* was Pard?

He was supposed to be her constant companion *at all times*. Wasn't this *a time*? Didn't *all times* include *this time*? If she could have crossed her wings and tapped her foot, she would have, but—but—but—TUMBLEWEED!

How would she ever get back to her babies? Wims. Beulah. Best babies ever in the history of the universe and the solar system and the galaxy.

Thank goodness for Zada. In her heart of hearts, Perlita knew that Zada would do everything possible to keep the chicks safe.

But wait! Thinking about Zada, Perlita had a vague memory that popped up. There was something she had forgotten to tell her camel friend.

Something important. The *best* news, but what was it?

Just then the wind pushed her again. The tumbleweed tumbled. Over and over. Up. Down. Then it bounced-bounced-bounced. Faceup. Face-down. Bump-bump-bump. Ouch ouch ouch!

Pard! She needed Pard.

American kestrels are known for their brilliant cries—*klee! Killy, killy. Klee.*

But trapped as she was, the only cries that Perlita could make were deep inside, where her tiny heart was beating as fast as it could.

# Rio Grande Banks

## 1868

Stories, my birditos, come in all shapes and sizes. Some are long. Some are short. Some make us smile and others make us . . . well . . . a little weepy. And then there are stories that leave us with an open-ended question. . . .

Zada and Asiye and the rest of the camel caravan transported goods and people to and from central Texas to southern California, in all kinds of weather and during every season.

But in the midst of all their traversing came a

devastating war, the American Civil War. In fact, all wars are devastating. So much destruction. So much despair.

Fortunately, the camels weren't part of it. While the battles were raging elsewhere, they were safely ensconced in their home base at Camp Verde. It seems that no one in the United States Army realized that camels had served in militaries for millennia, including the mighty forces of Afghanistan, to the firece fighters of Zanzibar. From A to Z, they had proven their valor, often at terrible risk.

Lucky for Zada and Asiye and the others, they were largely left to graze and gambol and generally take life easy, with the exception of an occasional field trip to the border areas, or to carry a bundle of mail to an outpost farther west.

When the war finally ended, the army decided that the camels were no longer needed. One by one, they were auctioned off. Some were sold to zoos or traveling circuses. Others were sold to miners and prospectors. At least a couple were sent to the gold mines in northern California, and some wound up as far north as Vancouver. Yes. That is a fact.

Soon, the larger herd of thirty-four became a smaller herd, and smaller yet, until there were only the nine left: Asiye. Halime. Naime. Rezan. Tarkan. Kahraman. Elif. Melek. Zada. The Pasha's elite camels. At least they were still all together. Teodor saw to it.

But as the weeks and months passed, one after another, Teodor had to find new homes for them. One by one, the camels sang out, "Güle güle!" until only two were left: Zada and Asiye.

And then . . .

Zada remembered that day as if it just happened. They were on their way back from Fort Tejon in California when Teodor, riding a mule named Lucille, announced, "I have something special for my racing camels."

*Racing!* Teodor had said *racing.* Zada did a

little dance. She had not raced in years and years. She looked at Asiye. Asiye looked at her. They could feel the excitement down to their toes. Zada lifted her knees. Asiye began to sway. Sure enough, as she always did when she was happy, Asiye burst into song, so of course, so did Zada. The camelujah chorus commenced; their joyful tune echoed amidst the rocks and rills.

Teodor led the two of them off the trail. First he relieved them of their packs. Then he and Lucille guided them to a bend in the river, the one called the Rio Grande.

"I found the perfect place for you to run again," he said. And he had.

As Zada recounted her story to Wims and Beulah, she remembered how the soft sand along the banks felt cool to her feet. She remembered the way the eagle caught the air currents and flew in circles above their heads. She noticed the purple blossoms on the sagebrush and the darting movements of a chaparral, so much the color of the lechuguilla plants that she was hard to spot until she zigzagged from plant to plant. So much like the jerboa in the nursery barn, Zada thought.

She also remembered the tenderness in Teodor's palms as he rubbed their cheeks. She gave him a nudge with her nose. He was her favorite of the People species. Asiye did the same. It was how they said *thank you*, after all.

And in return, "Güzel develer," he told them, in his quietest voice, a voice filled with cracks. "Güzel develer," he said again.

Zada wondered why he was so sad, what with the day so clear and the sand so cool? What was there to be sad about? Then he did something surprising. He slipped off their halters, the ones with the bells that he had made especially for them. "I'll keep these for you," he said, "just in case." Which should have sounded funny to Zada, but she was so ready to run, she paid it no mind.

Then he pointed out the long stretch of sandy banks, so perfect for a long gallop. *Ahh,* the two camels thought. *At last!* It had been such a long time. Yes, there had been a trot here and there, but a run, stretching out and racing, their feet barely touching the ground? The long, sandy beach was perfect.

Zada looked at Asiye. "Do you remember the rules?" she asked.

"Of course!" Asiye nudged Zada with her nose. "No bumping. No side-kicks. And above all . . ."

"No spitting!" said Zada, which caused an intense round of snorting.

They were ready.

"So ready," said Zada.

"Beyond ready," said Asiye.

Teodor stepped back and gave a whistle. "En parlak yildiz ol," shouted the two. And just like that, off they went, heads reaching forward, legs stretched out. The two of them flew down the banks of that river. And oh, it felt wonderful, the air crisp and bright, the beach all theirs. They ran and ran and ran, who knows how far, with nobody to rein them in, they just kept going . . . and going . . . until finally, exhausted, they had to stop. Their sides heaved, their legs ached. But none of that mattered.

It was the best race of their lives.

"I think we flew!" said Zada.

"We definitely flew," added Asiye.

But what Zada and Asiye didn't see: while they were racing, Teodor and Lucille slipped away, leaving two of the Pasha's elite racing camels there on the sandy banks of the Rio Grande. Above their heads, the eagle sailed atop the air currents. The sun settled on their backs like a saddle. And nary a trace of their matching bells could be heard.

# 38

## Rio Grande Banks

### 1868

What Zada and Asiye didn't know, what they couldn't know, was that Teodor had, by setting them loose, saved their lives. For a long time after the Civil War, when the camels were being sold and auctioned, Teodor had managed to keep the Pasha's herd together. He even gave up his small salary to hold on to them. But at last, the US Army lost its patience. He could no longer protect them from the auction block, and he knew that the life in front of them, as beasts of burden—or worse—might not be kind.

If he could have bought them, he would have, but he had not the funds to purchase nine camels. He couldn't even purchase two of them. Not even one.

So he concocted a plan. Maybe if he released them into the desert, two or three at a time, the army would not notice their dwindling numbers before they were all safely gone. It wasn't a perfect plan, by any stretch of the imagination, but it was all he had.

With each release, he told his officers a different tale: they had been kidnapped along the way, they had fallen off the side of a cliff, they had gotten caught in a current while crossing the river. Slowly, he set the Pasha's camels free, and he hoped like crazy that they would keep each other safe. Zada and Asiye never knew the truth of the matter, never heard his tearful güle güle, never knew his heart was broken, again and again and again.

They didn't realize that he had taken off

their halters with the chiming bells in order to keep them from getting caught on a branch, or captured by someone who might not be kind to them. He removed the bells and tied them to a cord, which he wore around his neck for the rest of his life.

No. All Zada and Asiye knew was that they had lost him, and no matter how hard they looked, they never found Teodor again.

But that didn't keep them from looking. It didn't keep them from hoping for a miracle.

**39**

## Anywhere

Some think of a miracle as simply *coincidence*. Others put it in the good old-fashioned *luck* category.

But at its most basic, what it boils down to is something along the lines of "a good thing happens at the exact moment it is needed."

# The Escarpment

## 1910

The dark began to lift, and with the light came the smallest flicker of happiness at the prospect of leaving the den. But first, Zada had to get back on her feet. They'd been too lucky—Zada couldn't press that luck any further. Pecos de Leon was likely just as eager for the dust to lift as they were, eager to come back to his den just like they were eager to leave for the Mission! Why, he could be on his way right now.

Zada wasn't so worried about herself. At least,

not too worried. (Well, maybe a little worried.) Years ago, she had made a bargain of sorts with Pecos de Leon, but it wasn't necessarily a bargain that could be relied upon.

She had to get up.

"Hold on tight, peepers," she told Wims and Beulah. "We are rising to the occasion." And slowly, oh so slowly, Zada raised her back legs. Then she pushed up with her front legs, all the while trying to keep her head and neck steady.

Up . . . up . . . up . . .

"Oof," said Zada. Every square inch of her was shaky. And achy. And sore. Nevertheless . . . victory!

But it was short-lived, because all at once, there was a flurry of flapping. First the chicks switched places. Then they switched again. And once more.

Then Beulah announced, in a surprisingly authoritative voice, "Do not cross this line." Which led Wims to ask, "What line?"

"The invisible line," warned Beulah. "The one I drew with my toe." She added, "You keep your toes on that side, and I'll keep my toes on this side."

"I don't see a line," said Wims.

"It's right here," replied Beulah.

Zada could feel a talon being dragged down the center of her forehead. It might be invisible, but she could certainly tell it was there.

"I see it!" said Wims. He did a little hoppity-hop-hop and then *Peck!*

"Ouch!" said Beulah. "You crossed the line."

"You said no toes, not no beaks," said Wims.

Zada could feel the steam coming off Beulah. Sure enough, *peck peck peck.* And just like that, the chicks launched into a furious round of *Peep-peeppeeppeeppeeppeeppeeppeeppeeppeeppeeppeep-peeppeeppeeppeeppeeppeeppeep!*

Zada took a deep breath, but just as she was about to say, *Please don't make me count to ten,* Beulah said, "Look! I can see shadows."

"Me too!" said Wims.

Zada peered toward the opening. Despite the thick air, for the first time in hours, she could actually detect some boulders and some lumps that she was fairly sure had been shrubs, but were now mounds of dirt with a few leaves poking through.

But then Wims said, "Um . . . Auntie? I think that shadow is moving." That was followed by Beulah, "It's coming our way."

Zada's blood started pumping. She'd know that shadow anywhere. After all, she'd known him since he had barely outgrown his cubbish spots. Pecos de Leon.

All the whiskers on her chin twitched. Her stomachs roiled. She slowly backed away from the cave's opening, while sending thought beams to the chicks: *Please don't make a peep.* That was mixed in with, *No chirps, no chirps.* And added to, *Must be quiet. So quiet.*

A low-pitched growl, barely discernible, reached her ears, and this time it wasn't the wind. Zada took another step back.

Then another.

The shadow stopped.

If only Zada could draw an invisible line with her toe, one that would keep the mountain lion at bay. Alas!

*Grrrrrrrrrrrrrrr* . . .

Zada froze. The dust-filled air felt super-charged. One false step and it might ignite.

Over and over, she sent thought beams to the babies: *No peeps, no chirps, no klees or killys.*

The big cat took another step closer. Its elongated shadow stretched all the way into the cave, bumped against Zada's foot. Even though it was only a shadow, Zada could feel the menace of it.

The cat spoke up. "Why, Zada," he said, his voice raspy. "It seems you're in my cave."

Zada started to reply, but before she could even utter a syllable, Pecos de Leon started coughing and hacking and coughing and hacking some more.

Zada whispered frantically to her charges,

"Please, please, a thousand pleases, do not let out a single peep."

As it turned out, she didn't really have to, because birds tend to hatch from their shells knowing that cats of any type—domestic, Himalayan, saber-toothed, Scottish fold—are their mortal enemies. Even tiny kestrels know the consequences of making their appearances known to a cat, especially if they are within the cat's swatting range, which our kestrels most decidedly were.

Still, they had a hard time holding in the klees and killys when Pecos de Leon, after a furious storm of continuous hacking and coughing, finally hocked up the world's biggest hairball.

*Don't laugh, kestrelets. DO NOT LAUGH.* Zada hoped the babies would pick up on her message. Because let's face it, the worst thing you can do to a cat is embarrass it.

# The Escarpment

**1910**

And how, birderoos, how would Zada know that? It does seem odd that a camel and a mountain lion would have what we would call a "reckoning." Zada was much older than the lion, even though at ten revolutions around the sun, the years were beginning to show on the big cat, too. His teeth certainly weren't what they once had been, and he was actually missing a few, having bitten down on an extremely tough bone from an elk he had once dined upon.

He hardly ever ate elk anymore, subsisting instead on chuckwallas and the occasional jackrabbit. Only once in a while did he manage to sneak up on an unsuspecting bird, maybe a quail or a dove, one of those ground-nesting types. He preferred lizards and rabbits to the feathered foods.

Still, none of this meant that he wasn't dangerous.

And besides, Pecos de Leon had not always been so demure when it came to his prey. In his prime, he had taken trophies for his crafty stealth maneuvers; he was known far and wide for his pouncing skills, when he would spot an unsuspecting pack rat from ten feet away, then *boom!* Four paws off the ground and no more pack rat.

Even snakes weren't safe from his stalking prowess. He liked their spicy flavor.

Nevertheless, what could explain the lion's restraint when it came to not chowing down on a camel? It seems like catching an old dromedary with creaky knees would be a nothing burger, especially for a master predator like himself. The answer, my birdlings, had everything to do with horses. You heard me.

The horses of west Texas weren't always a thing. In fact, for many thousands of years, there were no horses at all in the western hemisphere. Back in the Eocene, also known as "the Dawn of Time," there was a tiny predecessor known as Eohippus, which was about the size of a large Chihuahua—same skinny legs, same skinny nose—which evolved over millennia to eventually become Parahippus, then Merychippus (which sounds like a holiday greeting), followed by Pliohippus, and finally to equus. For centuries they cavorted all across the western lands, manes billowing.

However, all the models that were originally extant in North America slowly went missing. What caused that is up to conjecture. Like the early camelids, the mammoths, and the cave lions, it seems that the equine sort headed north and kept going until they ended up in Europe and Asia. And there they stayed until the fifteenth and sixteenth centuries, when some Spanish and Portuguese explorers, known as the Conquistadors, loaded a few dozen or more onto their ships and hauled them across the Atlantic.

As soon as the Conquistadors landed on the eastern shores of the South American continent, they unloaded their caballos from their barcos, reintroducing them to their ancient homelands.

Over time, some of those horses escaped. And so, for a couple of hundred years, these heretofore domestic animals became wild animals. And— wild or not—horses need a lot of water, so they tended to congregate along the banks of rivers, including the Rio Grande and the Pecos. They liked it there, and their herds grew and grew. The offspring of the Spanish horses became known as mustangs.

One day a young Pecos de Leon, not even fully

grown, decided that a mustang would be perfect for dinner. But as nervous as horses are, they are also pretty smart. It seems that they have a scout system, and as fate would have it, the scout horse, upon spying the young Pecos, alerted the herd that danger was creeping up on them. So, what did they decide to do?

*CHHAAARRRGGGE!*

Those wild ponies put their heads down and started running straight at the cat. An older, more experienced feline might have taken off on all fours and headed directly back to his cave, but we are talking about a young lion, only recently on his own. And fright tends to do one of two things—it either gets you going or it freezes you up. The latter is what happened here. Pecos de Leon did not have anyone to whisper, "En parlak yildiz ol" into his ear. So, our kitty boy was trapped by Fear in all its paralyzing wonder. Every muscle, from jaw to tail, was clenched.

What no one saw—not the cat, not the horses—

was the camel. Zada was just a ways upriver, when she felt the ground begin to shake. She lifted her head and sniffed the air.

Maybe . . .

She cocked her ears. Nothing. She waited.

Soon enough, she heard the hoofbeats. She broke into a run toward the noise, arriving just in time to see that a young mountain lion was about to become roadkill. It wasn't that she had any great affection for mountain lions. After all, a fully grown one could be menacing. But she absolutely could not stand the horses. And she knew that the cat would never survive the pummeling of several hundred hooves racing over him. Nobody deserved that, certainly not this cat who was just starting out in the world, who still had the last small tufts of his baby fur.

Nope. Not going to happen. Not on Zada's watch. She raced at the young cat, stood directly in front of him, raised herself up to her full seven feet, threw her head back, and hollered in her loudest, most death-defying voice, "*Baaawwwwllll!!!!!*"

A veritable fear of camel surged into those mustang hearts. It set them into a frenzy of bucking and kicking and whinnying and all sorts of mane tossing, after which they made a herd-sized U-turn and never looked back. They might still be running for all we know.

Lion—One.

Horses—None.

Zada—Victory!

And since that day, the lion, who became known far and wide as Pecos de Leon, had respectfully honored his side of the bargain to Zada by not eating her. And Zada, while only a wee bit worried about becoming the lion's dinner, appreciated him for his restraint.

You couldn't really say they were friends. But it seemed that they had each other's backs.

Mostly.

**42**

## Somewhere

**1910**

Speaking of restraint, Perlita was still trapped all by herself in her tumbleweed cage. The wind had come from everywhere. It had pushed her forward. Backward. Upward. Downward. Round and round and back again. *Seriously?* she thought. One minute she was facing the sky, the next she was facedown.

Stupid wind! Stupid tumbleweed! Stupid dust!

"Enough!" she tried to say, but it just came out as, "Thhuuphhh." Which just made it more stupid.

*Bounce bounce bounce.* Each time she landed,

every bone, every muscle, every feather noticed. The branches held her tight, like a spiderweb holds a fly.

She was beginning to believe that she was going to spend the rest of eternity trapped in its sticky arms, trapped forever, trapped until the end of time. . . .

Pity. That's what she needed. A big, fat helping of it. A whole mountain of pity. And where was Pard in this, her hour of need? Wasn't he her primary purveyor of pity? What was he waiting for? For chirping out loud, was he taking a vacation?

The worst question, though she tried not to keep asking it . . . and asking and asking and asking: *What about Wims and Beulah?*

Perlita sent a million wishes out into the desert, wishes for their safety, wishes for Zada to be okay. She even sent wishes to see her darling Pard suddenly drop out of the sky in front of her.

Of course, at the moment, Perlita couldn't see

anything. The entire universe was clouded with dust, dust that rose to the very top of the sky, blocking even the sun. Stupid sun!

All Perlita could do was tumble along, and hope like mad that this whole stupid day would somehow right itself. That the wind would stop blowing, that she'd remember what she needed to tell Zada—the *best* news—and that somehow, some way, they'd all find each other.

*Find.* That was the crucial verb. Find Zada, because if she found Zada, then she'd find Wims and Beulah. Of course, that wasn't happening until someone—or better yet, some bird— found her.

Pard! She huffed. *Get those tail feathers going!*

# 43

# The Escarpment

## 1910

As Pecos de Leon took another stealthy step toward them, Zada could feel the kestrels hunkering down, shimmying deeper into her tuft, following their bird instincts.

Even so, they were babies, after all. And following directions was hard. Zada had to get out of that cave before all baby restraint was tossed. The thick dust still floating around them was the only thing that kept Pecos from smelling the tufted twosome.

But then, to Zada's dismay, Pecos plopped down across the entrance to the cave, entirely blocking their exit. To Zada, his lack of motion was even more unsettling than his actual motion. She had to get past him because, oh yeah, there were chicks on her head, chicks that would soon become tapas if she couldn't get them out the door.

"Well," said Zada, as casually as she could muster. "If you'd just scooch over a bit, I'll be on my way."

Pecos didn't even flick an ear. Instead, he commenced to licking his front left paw, making sure to extend his talons so that she could get a good look at them.

Yep, the look was good.

She tried again. "This is a mighty fine cave

you've got here," she said. "But time to take my leave."

Not one inch did that cat budge.

"Seems like a good time for me to be on my way," said Zada.

Pecos stayed put.

She could feel the chicks fidgeting. Horrible thought number 292 popped into her head: What if they were so scared, they decided to try to fly away? All the chambers in her stomachs clenched. The chicks would just end up on the ground, appetizers.

If she weren't so tall, she'd consider jumping over Pecos. But the entrance was barely high enough for her to get her hump through as it was. If she jumped, she'd whack her head on the ceiling. She might crush the babies.

Nope. Couldn't do that.

*Thinkthinkthink.*

She took a hard look at the entrance. If she sidled close to the left, there might just be enough room between the mountain lion's back and the edge of the opening for her to slip past.

What other choice did she have? So long as the lion kept concentrating on his paw-cleaning regimen, and the babies kept their beaks shut, she had a chance . . . a slim chance. She sent another wave of thought beams to the chicks. *Quietquietquietquietpleasebequiet.*

Softly, one old camel slipped one large foot in front of the other. Hadn't she been on mountainside trails that weren't any wider than this passage? She could do this. Step. Step. Step.

*Quietquietquietquiet . . .*

Only a few steps more, and she'd be out. She could smell the good news, that's how close she was, and she might have been doing a victory dance in, oh, three more seconds, but just then, like a meteor zooming from the deepest reaches of space, the unmistakable sight of an American kestrel rocketed through the dust, directly toward them.

Pard! Despite his grit-covered body, there was no doubt who it was. Zada wanted to spit for joy, but the timing Could. Not. Be. Worse. In a rush of sandy feathers, he nearly dive-bombed the cat, swerved at the last moment, and landed on Zada's nose.

"It's me!!!!" Which set off a whole lolla-palooza of happy. *Klee, klee, klee, killy, killy, killy.*

Which was followed by, "Do I smell birds?"

And not for the first time, Zada really, *really* wished that she could fly. More specifically, she wished that Beulah and Wims could fly. That would solve so many problems, the primary one being Pecos de Leon, who was, at that very moment, sitting on his haunches, stretching his long front paws, and putting all his claws on dis-play.

It would take only a single leap, followed by a single swipe, and three kestrels would be cat chow. Plus, considering their perch, Zada's face might be added to the menu.

*And-and-and-and* . . . where was Perlita? Why wasn't she with Pard? At the same time, Pard picked up on her thoughts. He had the same question, "Where is Perlita?" Which, of course, set off a cacophony of questions. "Where is Mommy? Isn't she with you? Where's Mommy? I want Mommy!" *Peeepeeeppeeeppeeepeeeppp!*

*Focus, Zada, focus.* What she *really* needed to do was to direct Pecos de Leon's attention to anything *but* the kestrels. She was *not* going to allow them to become Pecos de Leon's midday snack. *Not!*

*Think. Think-think-think.*

And then, just as she had earlier, she could hear Asiye's voice, as clearly as if she were right there in the cave: "You know what to do," she said. "Tell him a story."

**44**

# The Escarpment

**1910**

Zada took a deep, dusty breath. "Hey now, hey now," she said. "Have I told you the story about a brave young mountain lion who rescued a camel . . . ?" The chicks instantly paused. Pecos lifted his chin, almost imperceptibly, which meant he was listening. "Yes, a very brave mountain lion . . . ," and she commenced to tell a long and highly exaggerated tale about a young, handsome cat who made an entire herd of mustangs stop in their tracks, mere moments before they pummeled a terrified camel who had frozen in fear at their charge.

"That mountain lion saw the distressed camel. He stood up on his back legs and let out a terrible *RRROOOAAARRR*. A roar so mighty that every single mustang in the river valley turned around and ran so fast in the other direction that the buzzards soaring overhead later swore that they sprouted wings and disappeared into the big, blue yonder, never to be seen again. Or at least never to be seen in that particular spot."

Zada finished with, "Not only did the lion make those horses turn tail and run, he also saved the petrified camel, who was so afraid she couldn't stop shaking."

She paused.

"The end," she added.

For a moment, there was a very long silence. Not even Wims and Beulah made a peep. Even Pard was extremely quiet. Finally . . .

"I love that story," said Pecos de Leon. And

with that, the old cat yawned. "Now, if you'll move out of my way, I'd like to take a nap." He took another long stretch, and then he sauntered right past Zada. And the next thing they knew, he was curled up in a large ball, nestled into the back of the escarpment, and purring like a kitten.

"This would be a good time to take our leave," Zada whispered. Whereupon Pard added, "To the Mission." He was praying that Perlita was already there. But he did not say that out loud. He didn't have to.

# 45

## Somewhere

**1910**

*Bounce-bounce-tumble-tumble-roll-roll-whirlwhirl-whirl . . . ouch! ouch! OUCH!*

"Ttthhepp," cried Perlita. Which translated as, "Helllpp!" It seemed like a million years had passed. She actually had no idea where she was—and even though the wind from the haboob had died down, the tumbleweed itself seemed to be gaining speed. This was largely because it had tumbled over the edge of a sloping hillside, and the downward trajectory, combined with the force of gravity, was tugging it toward the bottom of the hill.

Over and over, she rolled, top to bottom to top to bottom in a vicious head-over-heels cycle. Perlita tried again to call out, but to no avail.

She couldn't even puff, that was how stuck she was.

She was filled with if-onlys. If only that hill would stop sloping. If only her kilter weren't so off. If only Pard would come to her rescue. If all that happened, maybe then she could escape the confines of her rolling cage. And then, why, why, why, she'd fly *soooooooo fast*!

Well—that depends upon how you define flight, because what our kestrel mama couldn't see was that the bottom of the hill wasn't exactly the bottom. It was actually a ledge, and with the tumbleweed picking up speed, it was pretty clear to everyone except Perlita that she was about to fly, all right. But not in the way in which she had grown accustomed.

191

**46**

# The Open Desert

## 1910

"Hang on, peeparonis," was what Zada told Pard and the chicks as they left the shelter of the escarpment. Zada was hardly prepared for the thickness of the air. Visibility was barely three feet in any given direction. It seriously limited her navigation skills. And it was making her mighty thirsty, too. She actually couldn't recall ever being so thirsty. And if she, a ship of the desert, was this parched, imagine how thirsty the babies were!

Oh, she hoped that Mission fountain was working.

She was fairly certain their destination was in the same direction that the wind had blown, which should—if she was remembering correctly—take them in the same direction in which Perlita had been hurled by the haboob. Maybe they might find her along the way! If Pard had survived, then why not Perlita?

"Hang on," she told her bird crew once more, and with one foot in front of another, Zada, proud member of the Pasha's elite stables, stepped through the suffocating air, hoping like everything that she was on the correct course, and heartily, oh so heartily, wishing that they might find Perlita, and if they did, that she would be all good.

One thing Zada knew about Perlita: though diminutive, she was also puissant. She had survived other death-defying adventures, including once being chased by a particularly ravenous bear and escaping to tell about it. She had also been nicked on the edge of her wing by a diamondback rattler and still, after a long bit of rehab, was able to fly again. So the odds were in Perlita's favor. Zada believed that.

She lifted her head and faced north, following the traces of the wind. She hadn't gone more than a few yards when Wims piped up, "Are we there yet?" which was echoed by Beulah, "How much longer?" And soon their little voices were like a chant:

"Are we there yet?"

"How much longer?"

"Are we there yet?"

"How much longer?"

"Arewethereyet?Howmuchlonger?Arewethereyet?Howmuchlonger?"

At last, after the ten thousandth "Are we there yet?" she said, "Are you good for a story?" And not for the first time, it seemed that responding to a question with a question was a good answer.

## 47

# West Texas

**1870–90**

For millenia, there have been herds of wild camels in the world. There is a rare species of Bactrians in Mongolia's mountains, for example, that is extremely shy, allowing itself to be captured on camera only by happenstance. There is a relatively recent herd of feral camels in the outback of Australia, having originally been introduced to that country about the same time that our camels were introduced in Texas. And of course, there are wild camels across the continents of Africa and Asia, descendants of

Ice Age *Camelops*, gigantic camel ancestors who traipsed over the very top of the world from North America via the ice bridge and into Asia. They've been wilding for centuries.

But Zada and Asiye belonged to none of those woolly congregations. Before Teodor set the two loose on the banks of the Pecos River, right where it joined its bigger sister, the Rio Grande, he had always been there.

He had kissed them on their cheeks, which tickled. He had given them handfuls of figs. He had walked beside them, mile after mile. He was their personal person! And they were his favorite camels. Güzel develer.

But just then? Zada and Asiye were lost camels. No matter how loud their calls, there was no answer. Teodor was gone. Vanished. As if he had never been there at all.

From the banks of the river, Zada and Asiye looked out at the landscape, so wide and open, beneath the dome of the endless sky, a landscape that stretched and stretched, and despite the pair's mighty size, both of them felt smaller than the smallest horned toad. An expansive landscape has that power—to make one feel small, even someone who is big. They had no idea which way to go, or how far, or how long.

A big, empty, Teodor-sized missing made its way inside the two of them. They waited on the river's banks for days and days, hoping against hope that maybe he would return. He never did.

And at last, one early morning, well before dawn, Zada looked up at the starry sky, only to see the Chief Camel staring down at her.

She looked at Asiye and said, "I think we just go."

And Asiye replied, "Field trip!"

And as if the desert itself realized that two of its own had returned, after waiting for over ten thousand years, it spread itself out and welcomed them. It provided all the prickly pears and water and stars that they needed.

★ ★ ★

"Auntie, did you and Asiye ever see the other camels?" Wims interrupted.

"Not one," she replied, "even though we looked and looked."

That was true. Zada and Asiye, in all their many field trips—through the canyons, the arroyos, the high mountains—had kept an eye open for their camel compadres.

But no matter how far they roamed, or how much they searched, or how often they called out, Zada and Asiye never saw Teodor or another camel again.

"Not even Halime?" asked Beulah.

"Not even Rezan?" asked Wims.

"Not even Elif or Tarkan or Naime?"

"Not even Melek? Or Kahraman?" they asked together.

"Nary a one," said Zada. And for a moment, she felt her heart squeeze. She was old, very old for a camel, nearing her sixtieth year. It was unlikely that her camel friends had still survived. And not for the first time, she couldn't help but wonder if she was the only camel left in this big desert.

And then Wims said something so sweet, her squeezed heart nearly cracked. "Auntie?" he said, in his most sincere voice ever. "When I learn to fly, I'm going to look for them."

"Me too, me too," said Beulah.

And maybe it was a stray beam of sunlight that peeked out from the clouds, or it could have been that invisible drop of water in the corner of Zada's eye, but all at once, the dust in the air sparkled.

# 48

# The Open Desert

**1910**

As much as he didn't want to leave Wims and Beulah again, Pard couldn't wait one more minute to look for Perlita. The babies were safe for now. He used the bridge of Zada's nose as a launchpad. "I'm going to fly ahead and see what I can see," he announced.

You might think this would cause the sniffles. You could assume that regrets and sorrows would follow their father's imminent departure. But nooooo. Break out the sand fleas, because instead of the expected moment-of-morose, there arose such a clatter that Zada's eyes began to cross.

*Hoppity-hoppity-hoppity. Bippity-bippity-bippity!* The twins danced from one side of her face to the other. "Hooray for Daddy!" cried Beulah. "Let's hear it for Mommy," shouted Wims. Next, they broke into a *tap-tap-tap-KICK, tap-tap-tap-KICK*. You'd think that they were the original Rangerettes.

Pard did one last flyby, then rocketed into the sky. "I'll meet you at the Mission," he called. Zada understood. From all the way in and back again, she knew that Pard would keep searching for Perlita until he couldn't search any longer.

"See you there," she replied, with as much confidence as she could muster. She could feel the babies giving him a winged salute, their chests fully puffed out.

As he quickly faded from sight, the party

on the rooftop went high velocity. We're talking about a full-on bluster of baby-birds-gone-bananas.

Finally Zada couldn't take it any longer. Not one more *hippity-bippity* second! Her head pounded. Her ears rang. Her nerves were S.H.O.T. There was only so much an old camel could take. Wits' end was wits' end.

"Have I told you," Zada said, trying to calm the crazies, "about the conquistadors?"

*Whooaaa.* What?

Silence.

Long silence.

Blessed silence.

At last, she heard Beulah: "Auntie, are we on a field trip?"

Zada paused. "Why, yes, now that you mention it, we are on a field trip."

"To the Mission!" said Beulah.

"Hooray!" said Wims.

Beulah piped up, "Field trips are the best."

"Especially when there are conquistadors," said Wims.

"Yes," said Zada. "Especially when there are conquistadors."

# 49

## Somewhere

**1910**

Like a pinball, after flying off the edge of a very deep canyon, Perlita hit first one rocky ledge, then another, followed by a too-close encounter with a huge stone outcropping.

*Seriously? I mean . . .* Where was the bottom? Where was the top? *Where was Pard?* Every blooming feather was ruffled.

It was fortunate that the tumbleweed was springy, and that Perlita was light, because despite the height of the fall, her landing was relatively

Once Upon a Camel

gentle. And thank heavens for that. It seemed that in the midst of all the bad luck that had befallen her, that was at least a small bit of good luck.

And another small bit followed—in that last big bounce, the infernal tumbleweed had stopped its infernal tumbling and seemed to be wedged between a couple of large rocks. She wasn't moving, so hallelujah and pass the potato bugs.

She gave a little shimmy, wedged as she was, but *nope*. The tumbleweed was S.T.U.C.K. It was not budging. She decided to take inventory:

Feet? Sore.

Belly? Queasy.

Head? Achy.

Wings? Ouch.

Mouth full of grit? Yep.

Anything broken? Nope, nope, and nope.

Victory! (Sort of.)

And wouldn't you know it, the biggest win of all happened next because out of the gritty air, Perlita heard the best news ever—it was the sound of her very own name, being called by her very own Pard. At last! And finally!

About time!

"Ttthhmmeeerrree," she mumbled, her mouth still full of sand. But it was enough. The cavalry had arrived, and it looked a lot like a very determined American kestrel, who, if you held him in your hand, you might not even realize he was there, weighing in at a little over three ounces. But soon enough, you would know that what you were holding in your palm was Pard, cousin to the great falcons of history and legend, the gyrfalcons, the peregrines. He owned it. He started pecking away at that tumbleweed as if his very wife depended upon it. And she did.

# 50

## The Drought

### 1887

As Zada and Asiye explored the wilds of West Texas, they tried never to take the same field trip twice. "What fun would that be?" asked Asiye. "No fun at all," replied Zada. And wherever they went, there was always plenty of cactus to munch on, and an adequate supply of water. They never got too far from one of the rivers, or any of the small creeks that flowed through the narrow canyons.

But there came a year when it just stopped raining. In normal times, there wasn't a lot of rainfall in

West Texas as it was. But from 1885 to 1887 the rainfall was reduced to a whisper. As soon as the drops left the clouds, they evaporated before they hit the parched ground.

There was a small bit of water still in the rivers, but it had turned salty in the dry heat, heat that seemed never-ending. Not only that, but when there is little water, the river's banks become exhibition grounds for quarreling, and those quarrels are usually won by the fiercer creatures, primarily the bears and mountain lions and wolves. Though Zada and Asiye were large, they were still more prey than predator. In fact, they weren't predatory at all, with the exception of the occasional cricket, and those were usually eaten by accident.

So our camels went on the march to try to discover some other source of water. First they drank their fill from the brackish river, just to give them some time, and off they set. They went slowly, keeping their heads lowered to try to detect any traces of an underground spring, or maybe a lost basin that might accidentally hold some leftover rainwater.

Days passed and the heat grew stronger. The dryness started to eat away at them. Finally, after a too long and too hot day of wandering, their spirits faded, their bodies ached, Asiye said what they both knew: "We may have gone too far from the river."

Zada's heart sank. She had nothing to add to that. Instead, she folded herself onto the ground and waited for the sun to set. Asiye settled in right next to her, and soon enough they were blanketed with a trillion gazillion quadrillion stars. And there, just above them, the blue eye of the Chief Camel blinked at them. Together, they watched the Starry River carry the Camel Caravan across the sky.

Camels are made for stars. You will rarely find a camel choosing to live in a forest or a city or a swamp, or any other place where the sky is not wide open. Not willingly, at any rate. From their very beginnings, they have slept beneath stars. They've seen the Pleiades scatter their meteors across the desert floor. They've watched comets come streaking overhead, tails blazing. They've fallen asleep to the songs of star-bears, their lullabies soft in their ears.

That night, drunk from lack of water, Zada wished on a star, then lowered her head onto her old friend's back and closed her eyes. And while she waited for sleep, a small wind blew over them, as if it were tucking them in. "Tomorrow," the wind whispered. "Tomorrow."

# The Mission

## 1887

Zada's thirsty wish must have been heard by just the right star. The next morning she woke up, and there it was. Unmistakable.

"Water!" she said. Asiye lifted her nose and sniffed too. It was faint, but, "Yes, I can smell it!"

A thin thread of hope wound around them.

But that wasn't all. Floating atop the morning breeze was the ringing of a bell. It didn't sound like the twin bells that they had worn on their halters. This was a different bell. Much lower in tone and resonance, but lovely all the same. It seemed to be saying, *Wake up, wake up, time for a new day*.

Zada nudged Asiye, and slowly, the two rose, so thirsty that it was hard to get all the way up off the ground. Zada felt a little woozy. Maybe she had imagined the smell after all. She sniffed again to be sure.

Yep. There it was again. Water.

Zada and Asiye headed toward that wonderful smell, and to cap it off, the bell kept ringing.

Not five minutes passed when they came upon a raggedy old building, sitting in the very middle of nowhere, and there, right in front of it, sat a big, beautiful fountain.

The camels stopped. "Is it a mirage?" asked Zada.

They both gave great big sniffs. "That's water," said Asiye.

They took a quick scan. From the sad shape of the building, it appeared to be abandoned. But

just to be sure that no one was there, the camels called out in their most semi-melodious voices, to announce themselves . . . just in case.

This was obviously a people dwelling, and while Zada and Asiye were quite familiar with people, not all people were familiar with camels. Their most recent encounter had been with a rowdy group of boys, astride a rowdy group of horses. The boys and horses surrounded the camels, and for no reason whatsoever, started pelting them with rocks.

*Whap, whap, whap!* Ouch ouch ouch! What had Zada and Asiye done to deserve that? Nothing. That's what. So they raised their heads and bawled as loud as they could, and . . . well . . .

Adios, horses. So long, boys. Güle güle, rocks.

(Horses. Jeez, they're so predictable.)

Another time, the two camels came upon a sheep herder, with a straggly, scraggly flock of sheep. She was nice enough, but she wanted to clip Zada's and Asiye's fur with a pair of very sharp sheep shears.

"Not good," stated Zada.

"Bad!" cried Asiye, and off they went, as fast as they could, with the shepherd lady calling out, "Camel fur! I can make camel fur socks! Come back."

Zada would never forget her, even though at the end of the day, it seemed pretty funny. Camel fur socks.

So, people? Not so much.

Zada and Asiye were just as cautious when it came to crossing into some other critter's home turf, like the hidden mountain forest where the black bears raised their cubs, or the rockslide where the rattlesnakes curled up. And let's not forget mountain lions' caves.

However, because there was the small matter of them dying of thirst, they decided to take a chance here.

"Let's go," said Zada. In front of them was a low fence, but it was clear that the fence was only for decoration, because it certainly could not have kept anyone out. It reminded Zada of the prickly pear fence in Indianola that she and her companions had eaten. This fence wasn't one for eating, but it was just as useless.

Zada and Asiye stepped right over it and headed directly for the old fountain, which was filled with a large pool of clear, cool water. Fresh water.

You might think it was magic, like maybe the desert water djinn had left it there for wandering camels. But in actuality, someone had, long ago, connected a pump to a small, tattered windmill, and with each pulse of the wind, the pump drew up a cup or so of water from an underground stream. It made the water seem endless. Just what Zada and Asiye needed.

"You go first," said Asiye.

"No, you," added Zada.

"I insist," said Asiye.

"Good golly!" declared Zada. She couldn't wait another second.

Together they slurped it up. But no matter how much they drank, the fountain refilled itself.

Once their bellies were full, they stepped back. "I think that was the best water I've ever tasted," said Asiye.

"Same," said Zada. The morning heat had nothing on her. She was now fully recharged.

Renewed. Ready for whatever would come next. (Or so she thought.)

Their bellies full, the two camels took stock of the old adobe building in front of them.

There was a walkway that led to an arched wooden door that stood open, sagging on its old hinges. Right next to the door, on the left, there was a tall tower. A bell tower! Of course. It looked almost exactly like the one on the temple near the Pasha's stables, but not nearly so tall. Zada could see that something was engraved along its base: COR EST CAMPANA. SIT ANULUS.

Alas, she had no idea what the engraving meant, but she didn't need to read it to hear how lovely the bell sounded.

She looked up to admire it, and when she did, she saw a whole bevy of Mexican free-tailed bats, sleeping upside down underneath the tower's eaves.

"I'm glad we didn't wake them up," whispered Asiye.

"Me too," said Zada. "They were probably out all night."

Bats aside, it seemed the whole compound had been abandoned for years, maybe even centuries, because there was no lingering sign or smell of people that the camels could detect.

Asiye nudged the door open with her nose. Zada inhaled sharply when she stepped across its threshold. Inside was a large room with a rather high ceiling, high enough for camels to walk in without bumping their heads. Several wooden benches were scattered about and upturned.

The morning sun poured through the open windows and shone on the plaster walls. Blue, the same brilliant blue as the canyon sky on a summer's day. And the ceiling! It was a dome!

"Like the palace!" said Asiye. Even though the paint was faded and chipped, Zada could see the geometrical floral designs that ringed the dome.

For a moment, the camels stood there, memories of their homeland flooding over them. They could almost smell the coriander and sumac, almost hear the soft rush of the waves from the harbor, nearly feel the warm hands of Teodor scratching them beneath their chins.

Then Asiye broke the silence. "Maybe this is the Pasha's secret summer palace." To which Zada replied, "So secret the Pasha doesn't even know about it." They both chortled, because, honestly, who couldn't imagine the Pasha puttering around Texas, especially in the summer?

Actually, what our camels had discovered was the ruins of an old Franciscan mission, likely built in the previous century or even earlier. "Ahh," said Zada. She didn't quite understand its purpose, but she did sense that this big open room had, at one time, been intended as a sanctuary. At the very least, the fountain in front, fed by its eternal underground stream, had surely provided water to passersby.

Zada couldn't deny that this old place, this

falling-down, abandoned structure, with its miraculous, self-filling fountain and its ringing bell, had saved their lives. But despite the familiarity of the painted dome, there was something about it that made her feel uneasy, as if she'd been lured there by forces beyond her control.

*Silly,* she thought. Still, the overturned benches, and the sagging door, gave her an itch, and not from the sand fleas.

Asiye seemed to feel it too. "We need to leave," she said, but just as they turned to step out of the wide-open door, they heard, "Well, well, well, what have we here?" And right in front of them, blocking their exit, was a pair of conquistadors astride a very large, but clearly forlorn mule.

Introducing Cosmo, LaLaFitte, and Soot.

**52**

# Somewhere, West Texas

## 1910

Just then, something else made Zada uneasy. She had expected a hearty *cheep-cheep hooray!* at the introduction of the conquistadors, but as much as she appreciated their quiet attention, now the chicks seemed *too* quiet. She could feel them scrunch-scrunch-scrunching, as if they were burrowing into her scalp.

Maybe, she thought, they were just tired? Ahh, that must be it. Naptime. Of course it was. Didn't babies take naps? Lots of naps?

Nope. That wasn't it. Zada could feel their toes get tenser, tugging on the tuft, as if they were scared of something.

Zada heard it rather than saw it. . . . From the dense air above, a horrifying sound: *Pah! Pah!*

Hawk.

Zada froze. With her whole being, she could not move. The hawk cried again, *Pah! Pah!*

The chicks! Perched as they were on the top of her head, they were sitting kestrels. If the hawk somehow spied them—and there's a reason why *hawk*-eyed is a thing—there'd be nothing Zada could do to keep her charges safe from its enormous talons.

*Think, Zada. Think, think, think.*

Just then . . . because sometimes when you think hard enough the exact right thing comes to you, Zada remembered the tiny jerboa from way back in her baby days. She remembered his enormous ears, how they were as long as his body was tall. Most importantly, she remembered how he so cleverly evaded the sharp claws of the resident cat.

"Zigzag!" she said. And with that, her aching knees unlocked. She stretched her neck as long as she could and veered first to the left—step-step-step—then to the right—step-step-step. Left. Right. Left. Right.

Maybe the hawk grew confused. Maybe all that side-to-side made her dizzy. Maybe it just seemed too weird for words. Whatever. She flew away. When that *Pah! Pah!* was at a *pah-pah* level, Zada felt the tension in the tuft begin to relax. Her chicks. Her Wims and Beulah. They had done exactly the right thing. All their survival instincts had told them: *Duck!* Which was what they did. If she could have given them merit badges, she would have.

The feeling was obviously mutual because, in a whispery voice, Beulah said, "Auntie, that was awesome!" Wims said, "Best auntie ever!"

Together: "Do it again!"

But all the pride that Zada felt was only momentary—at any moment, that hawk could return, and next time, she might not be so easily fooled.

# 53

## The Mission

**1887**

Did someone say fooled? Of course, Cosmo and LaLaFitte weren't actually Conquistadors (note the capital *C*). Those guys had been dead for, oh, three centuries or more. And good riddance. The real Conquistadors had sailed from the Iberian Peninsula of Spain, on boats laden with livestock, including horses. They also brought with them special outfits made of metal armor, which were basically whole-body garb, complete with helmets. Even the horses had armor.

As soon as the Conquistadors set foot on the South American continent, their amazement peaked. First by the brilliant civilizations of the Mayans, Incans, and Aztecs, and the other residents whom they encountered, and second—and much more compelling for these greedy intruders—all the gold and silver that the afore-mentioned inhabitants used in their daily lives. They—the Conquistadors—became convinced that there was a City of Gold: Cíbola.

Legend had it that Cíbola was across the river to the north. Directions weren't exact, and there was a decided language barrier as well, but the Conquistadors assumed that the river was the Rio Grande, and Cíbola must be north of that. So they saddled up their trusty steeds and went on a massive trail ride, always in search of gold.

Once they crossed the Rio Grande, they found themselves in the desert canyon lands at the foothills of the Rocky Mountains. It was an arduous journey, and many of their number didn't make it. Not only that, it was soon obvious that there was no city of gold. There were plenty of other cities—the Zuni Pueblos, the vast villages of the Lipan Apaches and the Ute, the forest settlements of the Tonkawa, the homesteads of the Mescalero and Mohave and Kichai—but none of those were paved with gold. No matter how much those heavy metal guys yearned for it, Cíbola did not exist. It turned out to be a pipe dream, a myth, a figment of someone's overactive imagination.

They'd been, you heard me: fooled!

Which made the Conquistadors extremely angry. At least two of them got so mad, they spewed dozens of not-safe-for-tender-ears curses into the air. They stomped around, scaring their horses, who took off into the sunset, making the Conquistadors boil over, like hissing steam pots. Made them so angry, in fact, that they took off their metal helmets and dashed them to the ground, where they (the helmets) sat, undisturbed, for about three hundred years, serving primarily as way stations for several generations of prairie dogs and an occasional covey of bobwhites.

They might still be there, those helmets, except that one day a prospector named Cosmo, and his wife LaLaFitte, rode up on them while atop their mule, Soot. It seems that the corner of one of the helmets captured a glint of sunlight and tossed it in Soot's eye, whereupon he set to kicking his heels and braying in his loudest voice, launching Cosmo and LaLaFitte into the air and landing unceremoniously on their backsides right next to the long-lost helmets. More cursing ensued, this time in English.

But when Cosmo realized what he had found, he said, "Well, well, what have we here?"

He took his prospector's pickax out of his pack and dug the old helmets out of their dusty homes, shook out all the nesting materials from the prairie dogs and bobwhites, polished them as best he could with the tail of his shirt, and promptly set them atop his and LaLaFitte's heads.

"I think we are now official conquistadors," said Cosmo.

"I love being a conquistador," said LaLaFitte.

(Note the lowercase *c*.)

Soot had no comment. But he did notice that when the two climbed aboard his back, they were considerably heavier. Those helmets weighed more than you might think—a hefty five or six pounds each. Oof! Soot was not a happy camper.

It seems that old legends have a hard time dying. The idea of Cíbola refused to go away, and Cosmo had not only heard of it, he was convinced that he could prevail where others had failed. And LaLaFitte, completely smitten with her Turtledove (which was what she called her hubby), was not about to let him leave her behind in the small city of Presidio, while he wandered about in the desert. And besides, she knew how to use a pickax, which honestly,

Cosmo wasn't that great at, being more of a dreamer than a digger. Plus, Soot was a wedding gift from LaLaFitte's daddy, and she didn't want her Turtledove making off with her mule, either. Soot was a terrific mule, despite his penchant for tossing his riders.

Out in the wilds of West Texas, there were many ways to disappear. Take mountain lions, for one. There were also bears, rattlesnakes, heat exhaustion, flash floods, and a whole assortment of ne'er-do-wells who would steal a mule in a hot minute and leave you without a source of water or your boots. Or your pickax.

Why LaLaFitte thought her presence could keep any of this from happening to Cosmo is a mystery. But love, it seems, does that, it brings about all sorts of powers that you might not realize you have until you fall into it.

## 54

### Somewhere

**1910**

While we're on the topic of love . . . have you ever tried to untangle a tumbleweed? Have you ever seen one? It's basically an unmoored bush, with dozens of twisty branches. But Pard had found his Perlita, and by golly, he was going to get her out of its infuriating grip. He had to be careful. Pulling on one branch led to a chain reaction. He had to be sure that if he pecked at one, it didn't poke Perlita in the eye or jab her underneath her wing.

And of course, even though Perlita was trapped,

she was still Perlita, which meant she had to do at least a bit of bossing, which Pard endured because . . . love.

Yes. Love will get the job done, no matter how tangled up it is. Considering that only hours earlier, Pard had had no idea whether he'd ever see Perlita again, he would take the bossiness.

He also knew that the day was coming to its end. Soon the dark would make it impossible to figure out the puzzle of the tangled branches, and for his own well-being as well as hers, he could not let Perlita remain trapped in this infernal bush overnight. Not. Not. Not.

# The Open Desert

## 1910

Meanwhile, there was a problem: all those zigzags had thrown Zada completely off her course. Should she go right? Should she go left? Which way?

Surely the Mission must be close. She strained her ears to make sure there was no further sound of the hawk. Nothing. The sound of the bell? Only silence.

Instead . . .

"How much longer?" asked Beulah.

"I'm thirsty," said Wims. "I think my mouth is drying out."

"Mine too!" added Beulah. "I can't even lick."

"So is mine," confessed Zada, which surprised Beulah and Wims. "Even camels get thirsty," she admitted.

"We are thirsty caravanners," said Beulah.

"And we should be there soon," said Zada, but if she were being truthful, she might have to say that she hoped they hadn't passed it. Visibility was still low, and they were just about to run out of the small amount of sunlight they already had.

Unsure, uncertain, and unconvinced, she made an executive decision: follow your nose. Which was what she did. One step in front of the other, Zada could only hope that she had made the right choice. Though it was hard to tell time with the unnatural darkness of the dust, she figured that it must be late afternoon. Soon it would be even darker.

Something else: night on the desert floor could be cold, especially for chicks used to being burrowed beneath their warm parents, snug in a tree trunk for the night. Her tuft would give them some protection, of course, but was it enough?

"Cuddle up together, you'll be warmer," Zada told them. And saying that reminded her of curling up next to Asiye.

As if Wims were reading her thoughts—and maybe he was, sitting so close to her brain and all—he asked, "Auntie? Where is Asiye now?"

Zada swallowed. She needed to think about this for a moment. Beulah echoed. "I want to know too. Where is Asiye?"

Finally Zada said, "Asiye has been gone now for a very long time." She waited for another moment.

"Did she run away?" asked Wims.

"No," said Zada.

"Did the conquistadors kidnap her?" asked Beulah.

"Did Pecos de Leon . . ." Wims couldn't finish that question.

"No, no, and gosh no. None of those things happened."

Zada resumed her steady walking. Step. Step. Step.

"So, where did Asiye go?" Wims persisted.

There was more silence, only the sound of Zada's steps. Asiye had been gone for a long time. But how could Zada explain it? What would Asiye say?

*Ah,* thought Zada, *I know.* She stopped again, and in her most wondrous voice (because to her, Asiye was wondrous), she said, "Asiye, racing camel of the Pasha's elite stables, honorable camel of the US Army camel caravan, and loyal friend to Zada . . . she flew!"

"Asiye flew?" the chicks said together, incredulous.

"She did, indeed," said Zada, resuming her steady march. "Asiye flew."

With that, a whole chirp-o-rama of whispering commenced. She could only barely make out their words. The susurration continued for a bit, and finally Beulah said, "Auntie, how did she fly?"

"Yeah," said Wims. "Because Auntie, in case you didn't notice, camels don't have wings."

"Well," said Zada . . .

But just then, she heard the most beautiful sound in the whole ding-dong desert. It floated toward them. . . . *Cor est campana. Sit anulus.* The old bell's song was still just as lovely as ever. Once again, Zada felt saved by the bell.

She sniffed the air. "Water," she said. The old fountain must still be working. "Hold on," she told her winged passengers. "We are almost there."

And they were, but at the instant that Zada breathed in the smell of water, she could have sworn that she smelled something else; and although she only caught the briefest whiff, it was enough to make her stop in her tracks.

Figs? As quickly as she noticed it, that was how quickly it vanished.

# 56

## The Mission

### 1910

A resounding camelujah rose from her throat when Zada spied the familiar fountain, especially when she saw that yes, there was water in it. It wasn't the clear, clean water she remembered—the dust had muddied it. Still, it was something. She hurried over as quickly as her protesting knees would take her. But then, a problem arose. How could she lower the chicks to the water without them sliding down her nose and into the drink?

*Thinkthinkthink.* Then she tried this: she carefully splayed out her front legs, and keeping her head as level as she could, she lowered her mouth into the water, took several huge gulps, and then, with her long tongue, she flicked droplets into the air. They rained onto the little falcons. It wasn't so much that the water drenched them, but it was enough for them to have a satisfying swig. And a bit of a shower, too. In fact, it caused a fair bit of baby-bird hopping by the feel of it, and also some preening, which Zada wished she could have observed.

But then the babies' beaks started ch-ch-chattering, and she remembered why she was there: shelter. Here was shelter. So, just as she had so many years ago, she strode up the walkway and across the broad threshold of the old sanctuary. All the while, she sent out a message to the parent kestrels: *pleasebethereplease-bethereplease.*

Even in the hazy light, she could still see the lovely blue of the walls and the tall ceiling with the ring of faded flowers. And even though it wasn't a whole lot warmer, at least it was out of the path of mountain lions and hawks.

As if to verify that, the bell gave a resounding chime.

Zada sucked in the almost-clean air of the sanctuary. "We are here," she announced. Well, half of them, anyways. She never thought she'd get used to Perlita and Pard's flybys, but right now, she'd give a million plucks to see them coming in for a landing.

She called again. "Here we are!" She listened.

Beulah and Wims listened.

They all listened.

But the familiar voices of Perlita and Pard were not in the offing.

"Where are they?" asked the chicks.

Zada could only barely detect a bout of pouts, but before they could turn into a whole bushel of *Peeppeeppeeppeeppeeppeep*s, she stated, "Looks like we got here first!" Which ended in "Yay! We won the race!" "We are the champions!"

And it might have gone on and on like that for the rest of eternity, but then a miracle happened. Beulah switched from cheerleader mode to curious mode and asked, "Auntie, where are the conquistadors?"

That was followed by, "Do you think Soot is still around? I want to meet Soot," said Wims.

Then more questions: "Where are they? When do we get to meet them? Will Soot give us a ride? Can we see the helmets?"

The questions buzzed around Zada's ears, one after another. Where to begin? she wondered. She spied a very thin, weak beam of the disappearing sunlight; she walked into it and let it soak into her coat. It had been a very long day, and she felt the huge need for a good, long rest.

But what is a rest when there are so many questions left to answer?

Before she launched into them, she glanced

toward the open shaft of the bell tower. "Why, hello, old friends," she said happily. But she wasn't speaking to the tower. Nope. To the utter surprise of Beulah and Wims, a thousand squeaky voices echoed down the shaft, "Zada!" to the tune of the flapping of a thousand velvet wings.

"We've missed you," they said.

Wims and Beulah looked up to see a colony of bats, Mexican free-tails, hanging upside down, each one no larger than a mouse, and for about fifty-five whole seconds, the little kestrels didn't offer up even a peep.

In that near minute of quiet from the babies, Zada was able to let the bats know about Perlita and Pard.

"We will look for them," they said in a chittering that sounded more like: "Wewewewillwillwilllooklooklookforforforthemthemthem. . . ." As soon as the sun set, when it got dark, they promised to spread out like a cloud over the canyon lands. Zada knew that it would be hard for them, with the air still so filled with dust, but if anyone could find Pard and Perlita, maybe the little bats, with their echolocation superpowers, could.

"Thank you, my friends," said Zada. And Wims and Beulah chimed in, "Thank you! Thank you!"

And just then, the bell outside the door began to ring again, likely from the fluttering of the bats. It was like a cue.

"When will it be dark?" Wims asked.

"Yeah, Auntie. How long?" Beulah wanted to know.

"Is it time yet?" "How much longer?" "When will the dark happen?"

Uh-oh. Zada realized that without a reset, this line of questioning would absolutely drive her batty.

"All good questions," she stated. "But first, I thought you wanted to hear more about Soot."

And with that, two fluffy puff balls scrunched down into their furry nest.

"Ready," they said together. Which was exactly the same as an O.O.D. (Official Okie Dokie).

**57**

# The Mission

## 1887–89

"Well, well, well. What have we here?" said Cosmo. At first, Zada and Asiye didn't realize that Cosmo and LaLaFitte were people. The helmets threw them off a bit. It was their smell that clued them in. People have a very distinct odor, especially when they haven't bathed in a while, which was obviously the case with the fake conquistadors.

"Oof," said Zada. "Someone needs a bath."

"Agreed," said Asiye, twitching her nose.

Plus, Zada was fairly certain that she had

seen Soot roll his eyes, a maneuver that mules were known for when it came to people. The army mules were constantly rolling their eyes at humans. And also at horses. The mules didn't always get along with those equines with their flowy manes, so eye rolling occurred more often than you might think.

Zada immediately appreciated Soot.

So, let's be clear. The real Conquistadors, the ones who actually sailed from Europe to the Americas? They were unpleasant, scary people, and exceptionally greedy. They caused trouble in a myriad of ways.

Cosmo and LaLaFitte? Not so much. But they were professed gold diggers, which meant that they were totally interested in any scheme that might bring them some . . . well . . . gold, which at the end of the day was what the Conquistadors were about, too. So, when Cosmo and LaLaFitte found the camels inside the old mission, right after Cosmo uttered the now famous words, "What have we here?" LaLaFitte (who, let's face it, was the brains of the operation) said, "Camel rides!"

Translated: "We can make a fortune selling camel rides to passersby!" Because who doesn't want to ride a camel?

So, straightaway, the two moved into the Mission and set about creating their new business, which was a million times less arduous than using a pickax to uncover the famed city of Cíbola.

First, to the camels' surprise, LaLaFitte lassoed Zada and Asiye with rope strapped to Soot's saddle. It seems like that might be alarming, but considering that both camels had been brought up being harnessed, it wasn't as unsettling as one might think. LaLaFitte tied them to the old halter rail next to the front door, leaving them with enough rope to comfortably graze on the cactus that filled the courtyard.

"Should I be concerned?" asked Asiye, chewing a large chunk of cud in her cheeks.

Should they be concerned? Even though the conquistadors were people, they hadn't thrown any rocks, nor had they chased them with long, sharp sheep shears so she could make camel fur socks. So that was all good. But then Zada said, "So long as Soot seems okay, I think we'll be fine." And it did seem like Soot was well-fed, fairly well-groomed, and basically pleasant, especially considering all the added weight that he had to carry due to the helmets.

"I think we're okay," said Asiye. Zada nodded. Nevertheless, they also decided to keep their guards up, at least for a while.

And just to seal the deal, they decided to spit on it, which is how camels everywhere sign their agreements.

In the meantime, LaLaFitte sent Cosmo and Soot to the village of Presidio with a list of materials, including paint, so that she could make signs to post along the way for all those passersby who, she was certain, would die before they would miss out on riding a camel.

Presidio was an ancient settlement, constantly inhabited, first by the Jumano people. When the real Conquistadors cruised through in the mid-sixteenth century, they named it La Junta de las Cruces. A second wave of Conquistadors passed through in 1582 and renamed it San Juan Evangelista, and on and on until in 1760, the Mexican government turned it into a penal colony and changed its name to Presidio. LaLaFitte's family arrived during that time, and whether her granddaddy was one of the prisoners or one of the soldiers guarding the prisoners is lost to history.

Presidio had paint for sale, and that was what mattered in the moment. While Cosmo and Soot were gone, LaLaFitte, not at all afraid of the camels, walked right up to them and began to comb their shaggy coats with her own hair-brush, until they looked reasonably suitable for passengers.

Zada had to admit, having her coat brushed

felt nice. She even liked the way LaLaFitte hummed in time to her strokes. Her voice was surprisingly deep, and not at all horrible.

Asiye agreed. When LaLaFitte was done, the two camels admired the way each other looked.

"Your coat looks positively shiny," Asiye said.

"Your coat looks unequivocally radiant!" Zada replied.

And it seems like they might have chortled just a bit, because really? Unequivocally? Who says that? But instead, a fleeting memory of Teodor slipped between them. The last time anyone had brushed them, it had been Teodor. LaLaFitte was nothing like their beloved cameleer, but her steady, even brushstrokes reminded them of him nonetheless. Zada reached over and gently nudged Asiye with her nose. Asiye nudged back.

Teodor. A long time had passed since they had seen him. Years even. But they missed him anyways.

Then Asiye piped up, "Maybe he will hear about the camel rides and come find us."

Zada raised her head. "It could happen." And a small bit of maybe rose up from her very center and hung on. Unequivocally.

The day after her Turtledove returned with the supplies, LaLaFitte painted *Camel Rides* on every boulder in the vicinity, underneath which she painted *Like the Wise Men*. That, she thought, would be a great selling point, because who wouldn't want to be like the Wise Men?

"Exactly," she said, her face and helmet splattered with paint. And if the riders brought gifts, even better, especially if those gifts were gold coins. The Frankincense and Myrrh, whatever those were, didn't count. Gold was the goal.

While LaLaFitte was busy painting, Cosmo was directed to fashion makeshift saddles from bits and pieces of materials left behind in the mission—like the old cloth that was once draped over the altar, its embroidery faded and dusty and spattered with a brownish splotch of sacramental wine. The cloth, though thin from age, served as saddle pads. From pieces of the overturned pews, Cosmo built two frames that became perches for all the riders who would rush to experience what the Wise Men had experienced way back in the day—a ride on a camel.

Despite the scruffiness of their outfits, there was something about the helmets that gave Cosmo and LaLaFitte a tiny bit of status. The helmets weren't completely unlike crowns.

Zada was of the most elite of camels, trained by Teodor. And she had her best friend Asiye, also of the same elite stable, as proof. She raised her head a little higher, and so did Asiye.

"Binicileri getirin!" said Zada.

"Yes," said Asiye. "Bring on the riders!"

**58**

## Somewhere

**1910**

Speaking of riders, let's not forget the ride that Perlita had taken in the tumbling tumbleweed. It seemed like Pard had been pecking at it for hours, and Perlita, though grateful, was more impatient than ever.

In fairness, it wasn't only that she was weary and achy and still somewhat dizzy; she also missed her babies. And Zada. She missed Zada, too. And even though Pard had assured her that he had seen them, and that they were all hunky-dory, Perlita wasn't totally convinced, especially when, to his utmost, profoundly regrettable regret, Pard had let it slip that they had all escaped from the den of the mountain lion. Trust me, if he could have smacked himself, he would have.

Let's just say that Perlita was nearing her point of no return. Beulah! Wims! Zada! *Best* family ever.

And thinking of *best*, she suddenly remembered what she needed to tell Zada. It was the *best* news! And remembering it made her even more anxious to get out of this infernal tumbleweed.

"Faster," she urged Pard.

"I'm doing my ever-lovin' best," he said, trying not to get cranky. A tangled tumbleweed is difficult to untangle, especially when it has an impatient mama kestrel all balled up inside it, and also when it is wedged between two gigantic rocks. Another thing of concern to Pard: What if he was able to set Perlita free only to find that she was unable to fly? From the looks of it, her left wing seemed somewhat askew, as if someone had grabbed it and twisted it. And of course, someone had, that someone, or rather some*thing*, being the tumbleweed itself.

And don't tell anyone, but Perlita had this same worry. Her left wing was decidedly sore. She was trying her hardest not to complain, but *ouch!*

Given her size, if she had to walk all the way to her babies, it would take something like a millennium. Kestrel steps are short. Minuscule. Even their hops are barely an inch long.

Not only that, but the waning daylight, all suffused with dust, was quickly coming to an end. If the kestrels didn't escape the tumbleweed, there would be new dangers afoot, dangers that crept about on four paws or slithered along like S curves, dangers that would love to find a pair of kestrels for dinner.

"Hurry," Perlita whistled to Pard. "Hurry."

## 59

### The Mission

**1910**

Meanwhile, back at the Mission . . . The babies couldn't help it—as soon as they realized that not a sliver of light could be seen, they broke into a chorus: "It's time! It's night! It's dark!"

Wims and Beulah, with their special falcon night vision, watched thousands of Mexican free-tailed bats launch themselves from the rafters and trail through the old windows.

"Bye-bye," the two kestrelets chirped.

"Byebyebyebyebabybabybabykestrelskestrels

kestrels!" And as promised, they spread out to look for Perlita and Pard.

"Promisepromisepromisepromise," they echoed.

"If anyone can find them, the bats surely will," said Zada, with as much confidence as she could muster. The very fact that Pard had survived boded well too. If Pard could make it, so could Perlita.

Zada could feel the babies' anticipation rising. Side-kicks and taps were gaining speed. "How long will they be gone? Will they hurry? How far do you think they're flying? Do bats fly upside down?"

She had to steer them off before the stream sped too fast to build a dam. "All good questions," said Zada. "But did I mention that there was a choir?"

Wait. *What?*

"Auntie, did you say a choir?" asked Beulah.

"Yep," said Zada. "Right smack in the middle of the desert."

"That's silly," said Wims.

"There aren't any choirs in the desert."

Wait. *Are there?*

"But what happened to the conquistadors?" asked Beulah.

Which caused Wims to ask, "Where is Soot?"

"Hmmm . . . ," said Zada. "Their whereabouts is a mystery."

"Is the choir a mystery too?" asked Beulah.

"Of course," said Zada. Because, let's face it, don't all good stories have a mystery or two? Otherwise—boring!

Of course the biggest mystery in that moment, and it was anything but boring, was: Where in the wide, open, expansive, ever-lovin' desert were Pard and Perlita? And right then, Zada made another wish: *Please, give us a sign.*

**60**

# The Mission

**1889**

Signs. It seems that regardless of the painted rock signs and the makeshift saddles, there just wasn't an enormous demand for camel rides in the canyon lands. Mostly, there were hardly any passersby. Once in a while, someone would be trekking to Presidio to buy supplies, or more likely, to visit a prisoner. On occasion a mail carrier might swing by. Rare. Exceedingly rare. Unequivocally rare.

Days passed, followed by weeks, with nary a customer. And then, one morning, a strange sound arose from the horizon. Voices! People voices! *Singing* people voices. The camels heard them before they saw them. At first, they were just specks in the distance, but as they rolled nearer, Cosmo and LaLaFitte walked out to greet the newcomers, who just kept singing until, at last, they came to a full-throated *"Amen."*

Bird-a-roos, what we had was a gospel choir, making their way to Presidio for a choir convention. There were three mule-drawn wagons full of at least two dozen singers. And all of them wanted some water from the fountain, especially the mules.

A kindly neighbor would have said, "Sure, drink your fill." After all, the fountain never ran dry. But nope.

Cosmo said instead, "One bucket of water for a Liberty nickel." (He failed to tell them that the bucket was leaky.)

When the singers hesitated, LaLaFitte chimed in. "Buy a bucket, and get a half-price camel ride."

Camels? It seemed the camels, and Soot with them, had ducked into the side yard. All that singing was hard on their ears. So LaLaFitte quickly fetched them. Well, you can imagine the surprise on those choristers' faces.

*Whoa!*

*Camels!*

*Real camels!*

*Like in the Bible!*

*Like the Wise Men!*

Well, the hallelujahs went around the bend and straight up to heaven. Soon Zada and Asiye were saddled and taking one rider after another around the circumference of the Mission. It was a good day for all, and when the choir left, their thirst sated and their hearts full, Zada and Asiye could hear their jubilations for quite a while, until they finally faded into the sunset. Even Soot, having caught up on the mule news, was not as grumpy as usual.

As for Zada and Asiye, they loved the riders. All of them were gentle; as soon as they dismounted, they took a moment to say thank you and rub the camels' necks in appreciation. Moreover, they seemed genuinely glad to be in the presence of animals who had carried the Wise Men, even though technically, those exact camels were history.

Zada liked the way they patted her; almost like Teodor had so long ago. There was something about them that made her feel important, like she and Asiye mattered, at least in those few hours.

And isn't that the thing we all want, to matter? When all the choristers were finished, when the mules had taken their turns emptying the leaky bucket, when everyone had taken a spin atop the camels, Zada was sorry to see them leave.

"Maybe they'll come back," said Asiye.

"Amen," said Zada, practicing this new form of Amin, a word she'd heard a million times before. She couldn't decide which one she liked best, but what she knew either way, it was the perfect word for ending things. She said it again. "Amen." And just to seal the deal: "Amin."

But aside from that one day of coffer filling, the gold mine that Cosmo and LaLaFitte expected to gain from their enterprise proved as elusive as the famed city of Cíbola. Basically, it was a bust. Zada had to admit that the conquistadors (note: lowercase) gave it a good shot. But without any more takers, there was no reason to stick around.

So, one night, while Zada and Asiye were bedded down, the conquistadors packed their belongings, donned their helmets, climbed aboard Soot, and disappeared into the West Texas desert. They didn't even tell the camels goodbye. The next morning Zada and Asiye awoke to the emptiness. They looked all around, but the trio was gone. Nary hide nor hair was left behind.

Zada wasn't sure whether she was sad or happy. The conquistadors had been friendly enough, but she had to admit that Soot was a decent mule and she would miss his eye rolling and his jovial brays. She could actually feel a small tear welling up in the corner of her right eye.

Just in time, Asiye, who always seemed to know exactly what to say, spoke up. "I think it's time for a new field trip, don't you?"

Zada swallowed. Then she said, "A field trip would be lovely."

The thing is, they had each other. They had a whole desert full of cactus to munch on. There were mountains to climb, and ancient sea beds to explore, where the wind exposed old fossils of sea urchins and trilobites. And always, the Camel Chief watching over them, his blue eye shining in the nighttime sky.

**61**

## West Texas

**1890**

Zada stopped in her telling, to take a deep breath. Her eyes were slowly adjusting to the dark, and there was a bit of a glow from the dust-covered stars. Soon, she hoped, the moon would rise and bring a bit of extra light.

It was getting late, and she could feel the babies leaning against each other, and then she heard yawning. And why not, they should be exhausted. *She* sure was.

But almost as soon as those visions of Dreamville

crept into her head, Wims chirped. "Auntie," he said. "What was the most exciting field trip ever?"

"Yeah," said Beulah, her voice stretching out. "Tell us about the most exciting one."

"Are you sure?" asked Zada. That was met with, "Yesyesyesyesyesyeyes . . ."

"Okay then," she said. "Ears open."


When you live on an open desert, you cannot avoid some stupendously hot days.

"Oof," said Asiye, on one of those. "It's hot!"

"Crazy hot," said Zada. The two were folded up beneath a rocky outcropping, trying to stay in the shade as much as possible. The dry heat shimmered like waves above the floor of the desert.

"It's too hot to spit," said Asiye. Which made Zada smile.

"It's not too hot to go for a swim," she said.

"A swim would be excellent," said Asiye.

They knew the exact perfect swimming hole in the Rio Grande's bend, so they rose up together, gave a shake, and off they set—slowly, so as not to over-sweat. We're talking seriously hot. I mean, temperatures were cracking the records. Zada couldn't wait to wade into the cool water.

But as the camels approached the river's banks, they heard a mighty rumble, which soon became a deafening roar. The ground beneath their feet started to shake. Rocks that had sat in the same places for eons rolled down the hillsides. Prairie dogs burst out of their tunnels and headed north. For Zada and Asiye, there was nowhere to run. Nowhere to hide.

All at once, like in the blink of an eye, Zada and Asiye were completely surrounded by thousands of longhorn cattle. It seems our duo had gotten caught in the middle of a massive roundup of beeves. Cowboys—all atop horses—were moving the cattle from the border with Mexico to the markets in Oklahoma and Kansas.

There were cattle from horizon to horizon, hill to hill, no empty spots to be seen, and no way to wade through them. Zada shook as hard as the ground. She couldn't make her feet move. She was stuck. Asiye was pressed against her. "What do we do?" shouted Zada. And then Asiye called out, "Rocks in the river."

Rocks in the river? What did that mean? Rocks in the river? But then Zada figured it out. She and Asiye would stand as still as rocks, while the river of cattle passed them by. As long as they stood there, the longhorns would flow around them, like water flows around rocks in the river.

Hours passed, there were so many bovines. As night fell, the dust from their millions of hooves became supercharged. And something happened that Zada had never seen before or since: on some of the cows with the longest horns, a bolt of lightning sparked from one horn tip to the other, *zzzzzzaaaaapppp!*

Introducing St. Elmo's fire.

"I'll never forget *that*," said Zada. And you better believe that it was a topic of discussion between her and Asiye, for . . . like . . . *eons*!

"Did you ever?"

"No, never."

"Me neither."

"Amazing."

Imagine, lightning striking from horn tip to horn tip.

"Spectacular."

"Stupendous."

"Wowzers!"

As for the swim, the cattle had muddied up the water so much with all their thundering, it took days for the water to run clear again. But did Asiye and Zada mind the mud? Not one dad-gummed whit. After pretending to be rocks in the river, what was a little mud? The rocks didn't seem to mind, so neither did they.

# The Mission

**1910**

*Klee, klee. Killy, killy.* Wims and Beulah gave Zada a round of enthusiastic "Yessirreees! Bravo! Huzzah!"

Not a yawn in sight. In fact, the busy whispers started back up. Then died down. Up. Down. Up. Down.

Finally Zada couldn't stand it. "Chirp it out!" she said.

There was a long silence. At last, in his most plaintive voice, Wims asked, "Auntie? We're wondering. Did Asiye grow wings?"

Zada did not expect that. Nor did she expect to be so moved by their questions and their *remembering*.

"Why, yes," she said. "As a matter of fact, Asiye did grow wings."

"But," she added, "maybe not in the way you might expect."

# 63

## The Mission

### 1910

Sometimes a story takes a turn, and the teller must decide how much to share. Zada realized that she wasn't quite ready to revisit the next part of the story.

And besides, it was so quiet just then that she thought the babies might have fallen asleep. Weren't babies supposed to sleep? A lot? Weren't they ready for bed after such a long day, even if the bed was the furry patch between her ears?

Zada was ready for sleep. Every hair on her hump was tired. Slowly she lowered herself onto the floor of the sanctuary. Unlike her lightning-fast drop in the mountain lion's den, this time she took her time. She eased her front legs down first, followed by her back, which she tucked tightly underneath herself.

Ahh. She felt a wave of relief roll over her. But before she could finish one complete inhale-exhale, she felt a fracas brewing atop her head.

Before she could discern what all the shuffling was about . . . "She's down. Now's our chance."

"You first," said Beulah.

(Zada realized that Beulah had scooched over, so that she now stood behind the camel's right ear.)

"No, you first," said Wims.

(Wims was now standing behind her left ear.)

*Shuffle shuffle shuffle.*

(Clearly, something was afoot. No. Make that two somethings were afoot.)

"Together," said Beulah.

(Oh dear.)

"Anchors aweigh," they said in a single voice.

Uh-oh, thought Zada. Not good. Not good. Not good.

All of a sudden . . . *Pppeeeepppeeeepp-peeeeeeppp!*

Zada gasped. . . . "WAIT!" she called, but it was too late. Wims slid from the top of her head to the bottom of her long neck, where he banked the curve, and then—*whoosh*—down her side he went—*PLOP*—onto the ground, and only a second later . . . "Incoming!" Beulah repeated the maneuver. *PLOP*.

Zada closed her eyes, horror filling her chest. No. No. No.

This. Can. Not. Be. Happening. Whatever she had eaten twenty-four hours ago, plus whatever she had eaten in the previous six months, add in her dinner from two and half years ago, it all clumped together and began to swirl in her triple stomachs.

She felt her lungs squeeze. She couldn't breathe.

*Pant. Pant. Pant.*

But then . . .

"We did it, Auntie!"

Wait? Didn't that voice belong to Wims?

"Auntie! Look! We made it all the way down!"

That sounded a lot like Beulah.

Zada tried raising an eyelid . . . but no . . . she couldn't look. She couldn't bear it. But then, "Auntie! Wake up!"

Okay, maybe she was dreaming.

"Auntie!" Maybe she wasn't dreaming.

She cracked open one eyelid. It was so dark it was hard to see, but sure enough, there, right beside her face, two fluff balls, doing a victory dance.

She wanted to step on them.

Wait, no, she didn't.

Okay, maybe she did.

Instead, she looked at them sternly. "Next time, a warning, please." Which seemed mild considering that hanging them by their toenails might be justice served. A whole zigzag of relief, anger, relief, anger flooded her. But soon it was all dashed by the high-kick routine—*tap-tap-tap-Kick, tap-tap-tap-Kick*, which Zada had to confess was nothing short of delightful. And who can stay mad at delightful?

However, even though they were inside the Mission, they were still vulnerable to ground-dwelling critters, critters who might enjoy a tasty kestrel for a bedtime snack.

And besides, there was the matter of bed-time. This would be the hour when Perlita and Pard would normally be tucking them in, send-ing them off to Dreamland, safe in their parents' wings.

Zada didn't have wings. But she had her front legs. They were folded beneath her. She could tuck the chicks between her knees. There they'd be safe, and warm, too.

"No arguing," she told them. And with her nose, she finally wrangled them into that knee space, telling them in no uncertain terms, "Stay put."

Zada waited a long minute. The chicks were quiet, at last. Maybe, she thought, this would be a good time to tell a different story, someone else's story, something about kestrels. American kestrels, to be exact.

"Have I ever told you about the fiercest birds in the whole desert?"

**64**

# Foothills, Chisos Mountains

## 1908 OR SO

It might seem like the desert, as lonely as it is, would be a quiet place. But if you pay attention, you will come to hear its many songs. There is the *chitter-chatter* of the pack rats. The *whoosh* of the river. The *knock-knock* of the ladder-backed woodpeckers. The *snuffle* of the javelinas. The fluttering of bats' wings. It's like a symphony of sounds. And always there is the wind, howling, piping, whistling, whispering. The wind all by itself sings a thousand different chords.

But of all the sounds, what Zada loves the most are the vibrant tunes of the song dogs. The coyotes. The wolves. The grey foxes. Whenever they raised their heads up and lifted their voices, it seemed as if they could croon the stars right out of the sky.

Each day they sang the sun up and then sang it back down again.

There was also the tune that Zada recognized as a victory song, a frantic melee of yaps and yippees, the one that meant, *We've got our dinner.* Zada did not begrudge them this song. After all, they had to eat too.

But one morning, she heard a different tune, more of a whimper, actually. It was well past sunrise, past the time of the coyotes and their friends. That was odd enough, but all mixed into the whimper was the wild sound of birds: *Klee, klee, killy, killy.*

Zada had heard those klees and killys before. *Falcon,* she thought. As the minutes ticked, both voices grew louder and louder, angrier and angrier. Finally, Zada couldn't stand it.

She turned toward the tumult, and with each step, the voices grew. Sure enough, just as she got to the top of a hill, she spied them. One coyote. Two American kestrels.

But to her surprise, it wasn't the kestrels who were being pursued. It was, instead, the coyote. A small coyote. Just a puppy. It was trying to tuck itself underneath a mesquite bush. Its front paws were covering its eyes, and it was shaking from nose to tail.

The kestrels, on the other hand, were all business. First they dove right at the puppy's face, then they swished by and scraped the coyote's ears with their sharp little talons. The coyote kept yipping and yapping and whimpering. The kestrels kept dive-bombing.

Zada couldn't stand it. "Enough!" she called out. She stepped between the dog and its tormentors.

"Truce!" But the birds ignored her. They fluttered around and finally landed again on the coyote's back. But what the birds didn't see was the coyote's mother, running toward them at full throttle, jaws open. Zada could tell that the kestrels were about to be toast.

"Fly!" shouted Zada. And just in time, the kestrels let go of the puppy's fur and shot into the sky, leaving a trail of klees and killys in their feathery wake.

On the ground, the puppy was safely in the paws of her angry mother. It was the last Zada saw of them.

She thought that would also probably be the

last she saw of the fierce little birds, but hours later, while she was taking a nap, she felt something land on her nose. Actually, she felt two somethings.

"Thank you," one kestrel said.

"You're welcome," said Zada. Then she expected the pair to fly away. That didn't happen either. So Zada had to ask, "Were you planning to eat that coyote puppy?"

And though that was supposed to be a joke, to Zada's chagrin, one of the kestrels began to cry. Not just a sniffly cry, but a full-blown sobbing sort of cry, a cry that soaked into her brilliant spotted feathers. Her partner, who explained that that was Perlita and he was Pard, tried to console her, but there was nothing he could say to make it better.

It seems that the puppy had come across their nest, a small nook in the side of a large boulder, and discovered their very first batch of eggs. The nest was within the puppy's reach when she stood on her hind legs. Beautiful, spotted eggs. Laid only a few days earlier. They made a quick breakfast for the hungry pup. At first Perlita was heartbroken, but then she was furious, and in her fury, she had failed to keep an eye out for the mother coyote. Pard, in his concern for Perlita, had not seen the mother approach either.

"This is hard, isn't it?" said Zada, wishing she had better words to say. But there must have been something in Zada's comforting voice that spoke to the utter sadness that both birds held deep inside, because in two shakes of a wing, both of them nestled into the fur between her ears and stayed there for quite a long time. Zada didn't complain. She was glad for the company.

It seems that grief can open doors—and hearts, too, if you think about it—some of which are unexpected. As it turned out, Zada needed a friend, and Perlita, with all her bravado, turned out to be just the one. Once she got past her sorrow, she regained her natural joie de vivre, which made Zada's heart lighter. It even made her laugh, something she had not done in some time.

As for Perlita, Zada gave her a sense of calm, which considering her tendency to be anxious, kept her from yanking her feathers out.

And Pard? Well, Pard was happy that Perlita was happy, and so it was happy all around.

And once the two kestrels moved to the cottonwood tree, Zada followed. The tree was much taller than the nook in the boulder, too high for coyote puppies and their moms. Just right for this unlikely family. Zada stayed nearby and kept a close eye out for any of the dozens of predators who might enjoy a kestrel as a tasty snack.

And in return, Perlita and Pard took up a big, empty space even though they weren't even one-hundredth the size of Asiye.

What mattered was that ever since that fateful day, when Zada rescued Perlita and Pard, the three have been friends. And not a moment of peace has ensued since. Perlita was a veritable warehouse of *klee*s and *killy*s, which she employed to their full effect upon the arrival of Wims and Beulah, best babies ever! Zada would never forget the day they hatched. It was a jubilee of hallelujahs and happys.

There was never a more attentive mother than Perlita, never a more patient dad than Pard.

And never a more doting auntie than Zada.

And all was right with the world, until . . . *haboob*.

**65**

# Somewhere, Texas

**1910**

Perlita's wing *was* extremely sore, but could a sore wing stop a mama kestrel from flying as fast as she could to her chicks? Pard had hardly pulled the last branch away, and she was out of there like a rocket.

"Hey!" called Pard. "Wait for me!" He still had a few slivers of tumbleweed lodged in his beak.

"Catch up!" cried Perlita.

Pard flew as fast as a falcon can fly, which is fast. But no matter how fast he flew, no matter how fast Perlita flew, they could not turn *fast* into *find*.

Because sadly, neither one of them knew where they were. The storm had jumbled up any landmarks that might have helped.

If you were standing on the ground, looking up, you would see a pair of American kestrels, beating their wings against the dusty air; you would notice that they were flying in circles.

Around and around and around they went. Higher and higher.

Where were their Wims and Beulah? Where was their beloved Zada?

Perlita called and called. *Klee, klee. Killy, killy.*

Pard raced after her.

The encroaching night squeezed the last remaining bits of light out of the sky, and with it, the darkness ate at them until all that was left was to find a rocky nook and wait until the sun came up again.

Perlita tucked her head beneath her wing. Pard scooched his body as close to her as he could. Tomorrow morning, a million years away.

**66**

# The Mission

**1910**

By the time we grow very old, all our wishes have either been granted or they haven't. Some stay with us so long that they simply become a part of who we are; they grow old with us, and might even turn gray, like our hair or our whiskers.

Others, like the one that Zada wished about Perlita and Pard, go flying into the desert sky, and maybe (who knows?) a passing djinn or a wandering witch or perhaps even a rock fairy catches it and decides to say, "Yes."

Zada's wish didn't get picked up by any of those magical creatures. Instead, hers got swooped onto the velvet wings of thousands of Mexican free-tailed bats. As they fluttered through the twists and turns of a nearby canyon, they spotted Perlita and Pard, clinging to each other in a rocky nook. And true to their promise, the bats sang out, "Ffffffffolllllllowwwww-Uuussssss!!!" and maybe it took an hour, maybe it was only a few moments, it didn't matter, Perlita and Pard flew behind the velvet carpet of bats, flew through the window of the old Mission, straight toward the top of Zada's head.

"Incoming!" cried Perlita, landing with a flourish. Pard was going so fast, he almost crashed into her. But as soon as they both landed, Perlita realized that the chicks were MISSING! Panic set in, followed by . . .

"Mommy!" cried Wims.

"Daddy!" cried Beulah.

At the sound of their parents' voices, the

chicks zoomed out from between Zada's knees, wings flapping, feet hopping, beaks chirping.

In the history of American kestrels, there has never been such a stupendous reunion of *klee*s, *killy*s, hops, and chirps. It was a free-flowing fiesta of feathered frolicking, all of which took place by Zada's side.

Has a happier wing-ding ever occurred in the wilds of West Texas? We would be hard-pressed to find one.

The rowdydow went well into the night, until at last, the merriment ebbed. Zada stretched out her neck, and she—with her kestrel family now transferred to the corner of an old bench—tucked her head behind her leg.

"Thank you," said Perlita. "I knew we would find each other." And Zada, her heart as full as a mountain spring, fell into a deep, deep sleep.

But sometime in the wee hours of the morning, in that floaty place between asleep and awake, she was sure she heard the *kllloookkll* of a familiar chime. Careful not to wake the kestrel family, she arose from her spot on the stony floor and walked to one of the windows. The air had finally settled, and the stars were as crisp and sparkly as ever. She gazed up and there, leading the Camel Caravan, was the Camel Chief, blue eye ablaze.

She was still tired. Every muscle in her old body ached. The top of her head felt bare without Wims and Beulah clinging to her fur. She had many more stories to tell them. Stories about jumping spiders and double rainbows and ridiculous horses. When a camel lives a long time, she has a lot of stories. At least a thousand and one.

She gazed out at the Starry River, streaming across the desert sky. There was one more part of the story, wasn't there? But for now, this one was only for Zada.

And Asiye.

It was for Asiye, too.

# The Open Desert

## 1900 OR SO

Maybe it was the spicy leaves of the persimmon bushes, or the tough blades of the lechuguilla. Could have been the tart fruit of the prickly pears or the refreshing taste of new vervain. It might even have been something in the water. Whatever the reason, Zada and Asiye thrived in their desert home.

And of course, being together made a difference too.

"Here we are," Asiye would say. And Zada would follow that with, "The *A* to the *Z*."

Nevertheless, neither of them grew any younger. Soon they were nearing their fifties, which is old for a camel. It seems like it was old for Asiye especially. Zada couldn't help but notice that she was growing slower and slower. Zada had always been faster than her friend, but it got to where Asiye took only a few steps at a time, moving as little as possible, mostly only to chomp on a fresh yucca or catclaw cactus or a tasty thistle.

It was fine with Zada. She was old too, after all.

But she noticed that Asiye began to have a harder time climbing onto the bluffs; her footing became a little less sure. More than once, she stumbled over a rock or bumped into an ocotillo.

"My eyesight is not what it once was," said Asiye. Zada nudged up closer, and whenever they went for a stroll, she stayed right beside her, a kind of seeing-eye camel. Friends do that for each other.

But then Zada noticed that Asiye's long neck began to droop. She had always held her head as high as her hump, as a prized camel is wont to do. But as the days went by, Asiye's head fell lower and lower. Zada told her, "Let's just rest." And they did, lowering themselves onto the ground, necks intertwined, heads resting on each other's backs, the Texas sun soaking into their fur. Once in a while, Zada would leave Asiye to find a bit of dinner, and only when Asiye was thirsty or hungry would she lift herself up.

She spent more and more time just chewing her cud and humming. The melodies she hummed harkened back to their days in Smyrna. They were lovely and soft and semi-melodious.

And then the night came.

It was a cool summer's eve, with so many stars that Zada thought they might block out the dark completely. Straight above their heads was the Camel Chief. Streaming just behind him, all the camel ancestors, marching toward the east, marching toward the sun.

Zada and Asiye were tucked into their usual spots in the sand. The song dogs in the distance serenaded them, and they could hear the invisible fluttering of the pipistrelle bats. It was a night just like so many of the five decades of nights that they had spent together, beginning with all their frisky gamboling under the watchful eyes of their mothers; then crossing the wide Atlantic Ocean, trekking from Texas to California and back with the US Army, and lastly, wandering the mountains and canyons and desert floor of West Texas. As they waited for the stars to rise, Asiye's humming turned into a lullaby, not unlike the one their mothers hummed to them in the camel nursery. Zada couldn't help but remember their baby days together in the elite stables of the Pasha, when the jerboa swatted at their tails. Silly jerboa.

Zada's heart was as full as the Texas sky when Asiye said, "I have to go, my darling friend." And Zada knew. The thing she was most afraid of—losing Asiye—was about to happen. Zada swallowed hard, then nuzzled Asiye with her broad nose.

Asiye lowered her head to the sandy floor and closed her eyes.

"I will always love you," she told Zada, as she drifted into sleep. But just before she left, Zada nudged her one last time.

Finally the sun peeked above the edge of the nearby Chisos, making a bumpy line of orange light underneath the deep, deep blue.

Zada stood up, and just then, as if they had hatched from the sun itself, a flock of butterflies, tiny winged rainbows, maybe a hundred, maybe a thousand, maybe a whole squadron, swirled around them, their wings like small motors. Then, as quickly as they came, they disappeared, and Asiye was gone, leaving behind her worn-out old body.

And Zada, the oldest and possibly the only camel in Texas, and maybe the whole world, too,

called out, "En
parlak yildiz ol,
my Asiye."

And Asiye?

She flew.

**68**

## The Mission

**1910**

The day after the haboob opened with a beautiful clear dawn. Under the watchful wings of their father, the chicks were exploring every square inch of the Mission floor. Zada had to watch where she stepped. It turned out that the daring duo could zigzag as quickly as any jerboa, making it hard to follow their movements.

Meanwhile, Perlita perched herself up in a cupola on the Mission wall and preened her disheveled feathers. She gave her sore wing an extra stretch. She had finally remembered what it was that she needed to tell Zada, and she did not think she could wait One. More. Minute.

She launched herself from the cupola and flapped to the top of Zada's nose, where she did a less-than-graceful landing. She gave that sore wing another stretch.

"Zada," Perlita said. "It's the *best* news." She puffed herself up.

Zada wasn't sure she could take any more news, even if it was in the "best" category. But she knew there was no stopping Perlita.

"What?" asked Zada. "What is it?"

Perlita puffed.

Long pause.

More puffing.

Long pause number two.

Puff-puff-puff!

Long pause number 8,396.

Extreme puffing.

Finally Zada couldn't stand it. "Chirp it out!" she said.

And Perlita, still maximally puffed, chirped, "I know where the other camels are."

Zada did not expect that. Wait. What?

"Are you *sure*?" she asked carefully.

"Of course I am," said Perlita. "I know where they are!" She went on to say that she had spotted them while hunting for food for the chicks, but before she could tell anyone . . . *haboob!*

Zada was speechless. Could there really be others? Hope climbed aboard her humped back. She had searched for such a long, long time. Decades had gone by, with nary a footprint, nary a spitball, nary a whiff of another camel. Her heart raced.

But then her heart went *whoa*. Surely Perlita was mistaken. More likely, what she had seen was a herd of elk or deer. Why, from her heights in the sky, Perlita probably only thought she saw what she thought she saw.

Zada blinked . . . and blinked again. . . . Everything she needed was right in front of her. She had her bird family. She had the bats and the blue fountain. She had the whole big desert, where there was plenty to eat and more to love.

What she didn't need was disappointment. She looked at Perlita and started to tell her that, really, she was good.

But Perlita was not having it.

"Zada!" she said. "I know where they are." And as if to make it official, Pard flapped onto her nose and said, "Zada, have you heard the news?"

Zada waited. "We found the other camels." And there it was: two birds versus one camel. Zada set aside her disbelief. *Maybe,* she dared to think . . .

"I'll wait here with the chicks," said Pard.

And straightaway, Perlita touched down on Zada's head, and the two set out. "Tallyho," they said together.

After the first mile, Perlita scouted ahead. Thanks to her sore wing, her flight wasn't exactly straight, and she had to make a course correction. Regardless, she was sure she knew, absolutely, where she was headed.

A long hour passed. With each step, Zada felt hope rise up, but the farther they traveled, the smaller it got. Her knees ached. Her neck began to droop. She couldn't help but worry that they were on a fool's errand.

Time after time Perlita said, "They're just past that bluff." But the closer they got to the bluff, the farther away it felt.

As weary as Zada was, she was also worried about Perlita. Shouldn't she rest her wing? And the chicks. Were they okay?

But Perlita would not be deterred. "Not far now," she said.

They marched on, even though Zada felt as old as the ancient camels who had once roamed here, over ten thousand years ago. That old. Soon, she knew, she would have to stop. The hope she held grew smaller and smaller.

Just when Zada thought she couldn't go . . . one . . . step . . . farther . . . Perlita burst into a clamoring of *klees* and *killys*.

There, moseying along an old cattle trail . . . a dozen camels, their copper coats blazing in the sun. They walked directly toward her.

Zada stopped. Blinked. It must be a mirage, she thought.

But no. "Camels!" chirped Perlita. Then she cut loose into a whole torrent of collective nouns. . . .

"A herd!

"A passel!

"A plethora . . . a parliament . . . a posse . . . A caravan!"

Zada blinked again, and before she knew it, the camels pulled up right in front of her, all dozen of them. They began to nuzzle her. They licked her ears and rubbed their chins on her old back. A welcoming committee. None of them were familiar to her, but they were all familiar anyways. And they were clearly glad to see her.

And then, from out of nowhere . . .

No . . . no . . . it couldn't be . . . could it?

. . . couldn't . . .

. . . could? . . .

. . . she heard a familiar voice. "Zada?" In front of her stood an old man wearing a turban wrapped around his head. It looked just like a tulip. And with him came the faintest scent of figs. Suddenly, she couldn't help it, she held her head back and, from the very depths of her belly, she sang, *Bhhhhhhhhhhwwwwwwwaaaaaallllll*, upon which all the other camels joined her, each camel's tune a little different, each note swirling over another note, clanging against each other, and so on until the whole camelujah chorus rattled the arches and canyons, bounced against the outcroppings and washouts, and finally shook the spines off the mesquite trees.

Teodor, his lovely face lined with a million creases, but the same face after all, his whiskers white as the blossoms of a wild plum tree, reached a trembling hand to her face and rubbed her soft chin.

"I never gave up," he said. And then he showed Zada the twin bells, hanging from a thin cord around his neck. At once, Zada recalled the many times when she was sure she had heard their familiar chime. Could it be possible that they had been closer than ever, and simply missed each other? "My beautiful girl," he said, his voice cracking. "Güzel kizim."

And she *was* beautiful, her coppery coat now faded to the same color as an almond, her ears as soft as silk, her heart as full as the ancient sea that once covered all of Texas.

# The Mission

**1910**

After their reunion, Zada and Perlita led Teodor and the herd back to the old Mission.

It seems that as soon as Teodor had set Zada and Asiye loose on the sandy beach of the Rio Grande, he had made his way to California. There, he had worked for a retired army officer, a general who had bought some of the army's camels for his own.

After Teodor's several decades of faithful service tending the camels—and also caring for the general's fig orchards—the general, in gratitude, gave Teodor twelve young dromedaries, offspring of some of the same camels who had sailed on the *Supply* with Zada and Asiye, along with a cutting from one of his fig trees. "Take care, my friend," the general said, and Teodor did. He tied the dozen together and began the long trek back to the Chisos, always on the lookout for the camels he had set free, hoping against hope that he might get lucky.

"And did I ever," he said, running his fingers over Zada's ears, giving them the first scratch they'd had since the choir had passed through on its way to Presidio, however long ago that was.

And all Zada could say was "Amen," followed in good measure by "Amin."

## 70

# The Mission

### EVER AFTER

So there you have it, story birds. All the news that's fit to print.

Everyone—camels, birds, Teodor—settled into the Mission. Perlita, Pard, and the babies—who finally grew their full suit of flight feathers—moved out of the cupola in the large sanctuary room and into a nearby mesquite tree. Even Pecos de Leon made the occasional stroll-by, just to listen to that story about the brave mountain lion who faced down the ridiculous horses and their showy-flowy manes. Zada seemed to always be telling it whenever he was around.

It wasn't too long before Zada noticed that the nights felt longer, merging into the days, and back again. She spent a lot of time snoozing, her creaky knees tucked beneath her heavy body. One by one, the younger camels took turns resting beside her, so she wouldn't be cold. She loved the tender way they nuzzled against her, tucking themselves as close as possible. They called her teyzecigim and licked her face and ears.

And just before bedtime, Beulah and Wims would buzz across her nose, followed by their parents, until they all four settled atop her head.

It was always the same.

"Auntie," said Wims.

"Do you have a story?" asked Beulah.

"So many stories," answered Zada.

Zada settled into her sandy nest, surrounded by everything and everyone she loved. Just above her head, in the night sky, she could see the blue eye of the Camel Chief and his caravan, marching across the Starry River.

"Well," she said. "Once upon a time, there was a pair of baby kestrels. They were the bravest kestrels in the whole kingdom of Texas. One day, they had to rescue their auntie from the moving mountain with the big, big, big behemoth belly. . . ."

As for the figs . . . well . . . against all odds, Teodor planted the cutting next to the fountain, and last we heard, it was still growing there, bearing fat, juicy fruit. If you can find the old Mission, you might find the fig tree too. (But you'll have to get there before the birds.)

Just saying.

# GLOSSARY

**Binicileri getirin!** (Turkish): Bring on the riders!

**Cor est campana. Sit anulus.** (Latin): The heart is a bell. Let it ring.

**güle güle** (Turkish): goodbye

**gurur duymalisiniz** (Turkish): you should be proud

**güzel kizim** (Turkish): my beautiful daughter

**güzel kiz** (Turkish): beautiful girl

**güzel develer** (Turkish): beautiful camels

**joie de vivre** (French): zest for life

**En parlak yildiz ol** (Turkish): Be the brightest star

**Teyzecigim** (Turkish): auntie

**unum et solum** (Latin): one and only

# AUTHOR'S NOTE

When I was a little girl, my grandfather told me that there were wild camels in West Texas. And because my grandfather never told me a lie, I believed him. So every time I traveled west, I kept a lookout for those camels, certain that I would see them.

I still believe that they might be there. After all, West Texas is a mighty big place, and there are plenty of spots where wild camels could avoid detection.

However, it wasn't until recently that I put a few things together. As I began researching camels in Texas, I remembered that my grandfather was something of an amateur expert in the history of the American Civil War. He read hundreds of books about that horrible period, and he was the first person to tell me about it—or at least bits and pieces of it. I'm glad he kept the worst to himself.

I don't remember him specifically mentioning the camel experiment during those conversations, but I can't help but believe that he would have come across it in his studies.

Without knowing it at the time, I had accidentally embarked upon one story after hearing another—both directly and indirectly tied to my grandfather.

And that is the way of stories, isn't it? One begets another and another and so on. And the stories spin. Which is why I named my storytelling camel after the most famous storyteller of all time, Scheherazade.

If you know that ancient teller of tales, then

you also know that she spun her stories in order to save her own life, and in the process, she saved other lives too.

That is also the way of stories. To save lives.

I've lived my life telling stories, largely because I love the wonder and possibility of them, but also because I believe in their power. Zada saved her little kestrels with her stories, just as we can all save one another.

In these days of so much anger and division, it's more important than ever that we take time to share our stories, which at their most basic level tie us to each other in fundamental ways. After all, we've been gathering around campfires and kitchen tables for thousands of years and doing just that. We are, all of us, story beasts, made to tell stories, built for them.

Like the little kestrels, we need our stories to create room for laughter and sadness, joy and sorrow, to help us make sense of the world, even a world that feels crazy and full of dust.

Go. Tell your stories. Write them, sing them, paint them, dance them. Whatever you do, be sure to share. I'll be looking for them. I will.

# SOURCES

For more information about camels and West Texas and Kathi's other books, you can visit her Pinterest page: pinterest.com/kappeltwrites, and her website: KathiAppelt.com.

# ACKNOWLEDGMENTS

My heart is full of gratitude for the people who took time out of their own lives to consider Zada's story. Their expertise and comments helped me so much. Lindsay Lane, Shelli Cornelison, Anne Bustard, Susan K. Fletcher, and Liz Garton Scanlon—thank you.

Merve Gencturk. I made a wish for the most careful reader, and you appeared. Your dedication and eye for detail made all the difference.

My agent, Holly McGhee, brought her wisdom and sharp eye to the campfire at exactly the moment when both were needed most.

Caitlyn Dlouhy, editor extraordinaire, you always ask the perfect questions, the ones you seem to find between the lines. How do you do it?

I couldn't be more grateful to Eric Rohmann. You brought the characters here to beautiful, graceful life, and filled them with love and joy. Thank you.

My Simon & Schuster family, especially Jeannie Ng, Greg Stadnyk, Elizabeth Blake-Linn, Justin Chanda, Alex Borbolla, Audrey Gibbons, Michelle Leo, Irene Metaxatos, Carlo Péan, and Valerie Shea.

Thanks to my darling daughter-in-law, Laurel Kathleen, who found some camels for us to ride. Patti Miller, my artistic sister. You inspire me. And to the rest of my rowdy, bighearted family, you are the reason I write, you know.

And of course, words would never find the page without Ken, my partner-in-life, my unum et solum.

The heart is a bell. Let it ring.

# READING GROUP GUIDE FOR

## Once Upon a
## CAMEL

## BY KATHI APPELT
### Pictures by ERIC ROHMANN

### About the Book

As the last camel in Texas in the early 1900s, Zada has lived a long life rich with experiences, and she has stories to tell. Without her beloved fellow racing camel Asiye by her side, she finds companions in a family of American kestrels. That is, until a dust storm blows their little family apart, leaving Zada with two tiny kestrel chicks whose parents are missing. Zada must harness the power of her past adventures to keep the fluffy chicks safe. Using her experiences and her stories—camel racing for the Pasha of Smyrna, crossing the ocean on

a boat, army missions, adventures under the stars—
she takes on one of the most difficult and important
adventures of her life.

## Discussion Questions

1. The story's action begins with Pard and Perlita
telling Zada that a mountain is eating everything
and is soon going to eat them. Zada cannot com-
prehend this. Why do you think that is? How do
you handle things you don't understand? In truth,
the mountain is a great sand-and-dust storm coming their way. How does knowing this change your
perspective of the situation? How does Zada react?

2. The author explains how a camel has adapted
to the desert, and how American kestrels are built
for flight. All animals have adaptations: evolved
physical and behavioral traits that help their species survive and thrive. Can you think of any other
examples of this? What about cultural adaptations?
Are there ways in which groups or individuals adapt
for their own safety, comfort, or survival?

3. As Zada tries to outrun the storm, she wishes she could fly. This is not the first time in her life she has wished this. Why do you think she has continued to yearn for this ability? Thinking about your life and the environment in which you live, what other animal adaptations would come in handy for you? Explain your answers.

4. As Zada worries about Pecos de Leon, she reflects on the fact that she and the mountain lion have "both traveled a lot of miles and traversed a lot of country. That was worth something." How can having many experiences help you? Do you think it's important to experience situations similar to and different from your own life? What might you learn from someone who has lived a long time and done many things? Explain your answers.

5. As Zada moves through the storm carrying the chicks, an enormous old tree comes down behind them. "The wind had yanked it up by its roots. A hundred years, that old tree had stood there,

watching over the creek, keeping generations of bird families safe. Now it lạy in a heap on its side." How does the falling tree make Zada feel? How did it make you feel? Do you think generations of bird families will be able to find a new home?

6. As the storm spins Perlita and Pard around, they call out, "'Keep them safe!'" This is described as the "universal prayer" of parents. What does it mean for something to be universal? Do you have knowledge, ideas, or habits that are universal?

7. Zada's and Asiye's motto is "En parlak yildiz ol." This means "Become the brightest star." What do they mean by this? How do you see them striving to do this throughout the story?

8. When Zada and Asiye are young and Teodor is grooming them to become racing camels, he visits the metalsmith for something special to adorn the camels' bridles. The smith gives him a single sheet of gold and asks him to take a walk and note the

things that bring him joy. What brings you joy? How have you come to realize this? Do you think we notice joy as we feel it, or do we realize later that we had a moment of joy? Explain your answers.

9. The three basic states of matter are solids, liquids, and gases. Water can take the form of all three of these in ice, flowing water, and steam. This makes it a very powerful substance. When is water important in this story? Does it appear to be powerful? Can you think of other substances that can exist as solids, liquids, and/or gases?

10. A haboob is a sandstorm with very strong winds. What role does a haboob play in the story? How do the animals feel about it? Have you ever experienced an extreme weather event? Can you ever prepare for a situation like this?

11. According to the book, the most basic definition of a miracle is this: a good thing happens at the exact moment it is needed. Do you agree or disagree

with this definition? Do you think all miracles are this simple? If not, how do you define a miracle?

12. When Pecos de Leon is young, Zada protects him from wild ponies. In that moment, they strike an unspoken bargain in which the cat will not eat the camel. What does this say about their personalities? Do you think these sorts of impulsive, unspoken bargains last forever? Should Zada be afraid of Pecos de Leon? Explain your answers.

13. While Zada and the chicks are sheltering in a cave, they encounter the old mountain lion. Zada is certain the old cat would love to eat the chicks, so she decides to tell him a story. Her story reminds Pecos of what Zada did for him; however, in this telling, she makes him a hero. Why do you think this version of the story lessens the dangerous situation? How does it affect Pecos?

14. As Zada travels with the chicks, they begin to ask questions she can't answer about when they will

arrive, where they are going, and how much longer they have to travel. She asks them if they are ready for a story instead, noting, "And not for the first time, it seemed that responding to a question with a question was a good answer." What does she mean by this? Have you ever responded to a question with a question? When might that be helpful, and when might it make things difficult?

15. As they finally near the mission, Zada sniffs the air and smells water. What does water smell like? What descriptive words explain the smell and taste of water?

16. While Pard is freeing Perlita from the tumbleweed, Perlita thinks about her family: Beulah, Wims, and Zada. Beulah and Wims are her babies, but birds and camels aren't related by blood. Instead, Zada is the kestrels' chosen family, and she feels the same way about them. The animals find a family in one another despite their differences. Can people do this too? What makes someone family? Explain your answers.

17. Throughout much of the story, Zada doesn't know where Pard and Perlita are. She refers to this as "the biggest mystery in that moment." Of course, this mystery is one that fills her with worry and fear. Do you think life's mysteries are sometimes too difficult to think about? What does she mean by "in that moment"? Will there be other mysteries for Zada? Explain your answers.

18. Read the description of the Pasha's grand home and grounds, and then read the section in chapter 51 that begins with "Bats aside, it seemed the whole compound" and ends with "geometrical floral designs that ringed the dome." What similarities do you find in these descriptions? Do you think there are many ways to be rich, and many versions of beauty and splendor?

19. Zada gives a description of witnessing St. Elmo's Fire. This is a real weather phenomenon that happens during storms. It is a blue glow that appears between pointy objects during storms; this

is due to extra electrons in the ground creating a powerful electric field that can break the air down into plasma. This rare phenomenon can be scientifically explained and understood, but does not seem so easily defined when witnessed. Have you ever seen anything natural that seemed magical or unreal, or was difficult to describe in words? Like Zada, do you remember that moment with the same wonder you felt when you first experienced it?

20. Stories sustained Zada when she lost Asiye, and they sustained the birds during their time of fear and hardship, including protecting them from Pecos de Leon. What makes a story powerful enough to sustain and protect? Which kinds of stories do you find to be most powerful?

21. At the end of the book, Zada begins a new story that starts with "Once upon a time, there was a pair of baby kestrels." Throughout the book, Zada gives her stories to others, including Pecos and

the chicks. Why do you think she does this? What do stories mean to her? Why does she start a new story?

22. In the book, there are illustrations of the characters and their environment sprinkled throughout the pages. What role does the artwork play in this story? How does the art enhance the reader's experience, and how do these illustrations add to the reader's understanding and connection to Zada, her story, and her friends?

*This guide has been provided by Simon & Schuster for classroom, library, and reading group use. It may be reproduced in its entirety or excerpted for these purposes.*

Turn the page for a sneak peek at
*The True Blue Scouts of Sugar Man Swamp.*

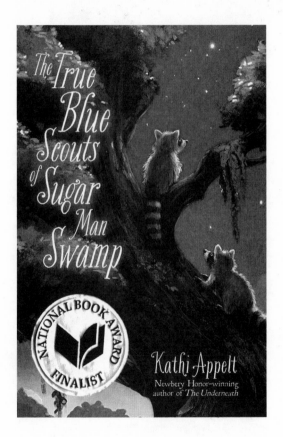

FROM THE ROOFTOP OF INFORMATION HEADQUARTERS, Bingo and J'miah stood on their back paws and watched Little Mama and Daddy-O trundle away; their stripy gray and black silhouettes grew smaller and smaller in the deepening dusk.

Daddy-O called out, "Make us proud, boys!"

That was followed by Little Mama. "Be sure to follow orders!"

For as long as raccoons had inhabited the Sugar Man Swamp, which was eons, they had been the Official Scouts, ordained by the Sugar Man himself back in the year Aught One, also known as the Beginning of Time. Of course, Bingo and J'miah would follow the orders. They knew them by heart.

OFFICIAL SUGAR MAN SWAMP SCOUT ORDERS
- keep your eyes open
- keep your ears to the ground
- keep your nose in the air

- be true and faithful to each other
- in short, be good

These orders were practical, and the raccoon brothers had no problem following them. Besides, Bingo and J'miah weren't *ordinary* Swamp Scouts. They were, in fact, Information Officers, a highly specialized branch of the Scout system. And because of this there were two additional orders:

- always heed the Voice of Intelligence, and
- in the event of an emergency, *wake up the Sugar Man*

The first additional order was easy enough, as we shall soon see, but the second was a different matter. The problem? Nobody really knew exactly where the Sugar Man slept, only that it was somewhere in the deepest, darkest part of the swamp. He hadn't been seen in many years.

The bigger problem? Waking the Sugar Man up wasn't all that easy. He slept like a log. Literally.

The biggest problem? What if he woke up cranky? Every denizen in the swamp knew that the *wrath of the Sugar Man* was something to avoid.

He also had a rattlesnake pet, Gertrude.

*Crotalus horridus GIGANTICUS* (also known as CHG).

Brothers and sisters, the stakes were high.

GOT TO GO WAY, WAY BACK INTO YESTERDAY AND THE yesterday before that, maybe a million yesterdays, actually more than a million, a *gazillion* yesterdays, to hear about the Sugar Man. Got to go back to when the sea had only barely rolled its way south into the Gulf of Mexico and left behind the slow-moving Bayou Tourterelle, which meandered through the middle of a wide, open marsh.

Sitting as it was in the deep southern side of the continent, the marsh had long days of sunshine and plenty of rain, all the right ingredients to give birth to a whole host of species of plants and animals. And like a tree rising up out of the rich red dirt, soon enough a creature born of the swamp rose up too.

He was taller than his cousin Sasquatch. Taller than Barmanou. Way taller than the Yeti. His legs and arms were like the new cedar trees that were taking root all around, tough and sinuous. His hands were as wide and big as palmetto ferns. His hair looked just like the Spanish moss that hung on the north side of the cypress trees, and the rest of his body was covered in rough black fur, like the fur of the *ursus americanus luteolus*, UAL, also known as Louisiana black bear, that had taken up residence in the area.

You could say that he was made up of bits and pieces of every living creature in the swamp, every duck, fox, lizard, and catfish, every pitcher plant, muskrat, and termite.

Of course, Bingo and J'miah knew the history. Little Mama and Daddy-O had made sure of it.

Over the years, however, the Sugar Man has grown older and older and sleepier and sleepier. Let's not forget that he's been there for too many years to count, since back before we even measured time in years. But just because the Sugar Man is old and sleepy doesn't mean he can't spin an alligator over his head and toss him into orbit. Nosirree, Bob. In fact, whenever he gets mad, he tends to throw things.

All in all, it's not a good idea to stir up the *wrath of the Sugar Man*.

More irresistible
animal adventures from Newbery honoree

# Kathi Appelt